THE SHOWERS

DYLAN SINDELAR

MILTON & HUGO L.L.C.
4407 Park Ave., Suite 5
Union City, NJ 07087, USA

Website: *www. miltonandhugo.com*
Hotline: *1- 888-778-0033*
Email: *info@miltonandhugo.com*

Ordering Information:
Quantity sales. Special discounts are granted to corporations, associations, and other organizations. For more information on these discounts, please reach out to the publisher using the contact information provided above.

Library of Congress Control Number: 2024911342
ISBN-13:   979-8-89285-097-1   [Paperback Edition]
                    979-8-89285-098-8   [Digital Edition]

Rev. date: 05/30/2024

For the teachers.
Cheers.

The following account was posted on an online
forum beginning in the fall of 2012.
The author refers to himself only as "Jack."
His tale centers on Broken Bow, Nebraska,
and a site called *The Showers*.
This could be a story about the horrors that permeate that place.
This could be a story about what became
of the man who witnessed them.
This could just be another campfire story.
I suppose that is up to you.

PART I

THE CAMPFIRE STORY

OCTOBER 7TH, 2012

In every corner of the world, regional folklore and mythology exist that refuse to fade from the cultural zeitgeist. Whether the stories from a given location center around haunted asylums on the outskirts of major cities, creatures that live in nearby woods, or ghosts that haunt desolate stretches of road, the tales often share a common and convenient characteristic; no one who spreads these stories has ever visited these places themselves, seen these supposed cryptids with their own eyes, or witnessed any paranormal happenings personally.

Members of every generation proclaim to know someone whose "brother's best friend's sister" went to the "haunted house with thirteen floors that used *real* blood, snakes, and spiders – the one that is *so* scary that no one has ever made it all the way through." The same storytellers swear by their stories without ever providing a single shred of evidence because "everyone *knows* the stories are true. They inevitably pass the tales onto their children, who modify them just enough to keep them timely, and the cycle continues.

I'm as skeptical as anyone when it comes to these stories. But I was a junkie for them when I was younger. I constantly scoured web pages, paranormal magazines, and the horror section of the library for any new and terrifying tales related to whichever area of the country I was living in at the time.

I spread stories about haunted pizza parlors in New York City that didn't exist, my imaginary cousins' encounter with the Jersey Devil, and how my long-dead grandfather encountered a feral, human-like demon creature in the mountains of Colorado, just to name a few. I even broke the core rule with stories like these: *never put yourself in them.* This took guts because it left me personally open to scrutiny; I had to make sure that I told them the exact same way to everyone who chose to listen, or else my credibility would be lost. My carefully constructed horror canon would be toast.

Surprisingly, I remained consistent enough that no one ever called my bluff.

I like to think I've made some frightening contributions to various urban legends around the Midwest and several towns along the East Coast. There was always a surge of joy whenever I would wander the halls at school and hear one of my classmates retell my stories to another one of their friends—adding little bits here and there like a massive game of telephone. I knew, of course, that the stories were complete fiction, but I stood my ground whenever I asked about them. I would ham it up with a bit of acting when I discussed them, speaking with a shaky voice or looking scared when I would recount a horrific situation that I supposedly experienced myself. It gave the stories a last little sprinkle of believability.

This mostly innocent part of my childhood led me to my current predicament, which I will recount in full for readers to take from it what they will. I have laid this little introduction out as a sort of disclaimer—aimed particularly at those who will call *this* story into question. I played the part of the boy who cried wolf for years, but I assure you, with every ounce of honesty and integrity I have left, that *the wolf is real this time.*

From my introduction, it is probably apparent that I moved around the country quite a bit in my middle and high school years. Neither of my parents had anything to do with the armed forces; they simply didn't tend to hang around any given place for too long. I suppose it had some sort of destabilizing effect on me, but it just generally meant that I never had the time to form any particularly deep or lasting relationships. With that said, I had a thirst for attention that made me a complete ham in my younger years. I made casual friends quickly, was often the class clown, and (likely because of that fact) was often disliked by my teachers. This never became a real problem, as I was usually in another state by the time my presence began to really wear on them.

The aforementioned friendships were fleeting, as were the few relatively positive relationships that I ever managed to forge with my teachers. Because of the following events, my memory of one teacher is biased. But I will attempt to present the least-skewed version of our unorthodox friendship I can.

Mr. Mays was one of my English teachers in the early years of my high school experience. Being an adult now, I have a better understanding of how horrible children are to deal with during their teenage years. So, I can honestly say that I have no clue how he connected with his students in the way he did, especially considering the mess of raging hormones amid our inherent generational disconnect. He seemed like one of us; he talked like us, made relevant pop-culture references, listened to modern music, and would sometimes even say *hell* or *damn* while giving a passionate lecture about a topic like Nineteenth-Century Gothic Romanticism. Something as simple as light swearing solidified him as *cool* in the eyes of a bunch of immature high schoolers.

My memories of Mr. Mays mainly stem from how deeply he immersed himself in anything he worked on. The instance that is still very vivid in my mind occurred on Halloween of my sophomore year.

Mr. Mays had the stereotypical teacher decorations hung up around his classroom. Smiling jack-o-lanterns and cartoon black cats with horrified expressions adorned the walls but went unnoticed by most students. On the 31st of October, most teachers rolled their eyes at the fact that teenagers still took dressing up in costumes on Halloween seriously. But, ever the people pleaser, Mr. Mays decided to treat our class to a seasonal story.

I remember being surprised as I walked into the classroom to find the blinds drawn, black sheets hung over the smaller windows, candles burning around the room, and a frowning jack-o-lantern sitting on a stool in front of our desks. Mr. Mays sat in his chair, patiently watching the students trickle into class and take their seats. Students were silent as they entered the room; they were either too caught off guard to care about petty conversations or too confused to remember what they were just discussing. We took our seats, and Mr. Mays began his lecture. He moved to the center of the room and sat in his chair next to the jack-o-lantern. He spoke quietly to set the mood.

"Today is probably my favorite day of the year, class," he said with a calm tone and deliberate cadence. "Halloween is my favorite holiday." He paused and looked around at each of us, candlelight reflecting in his eyes. "I want to share exactly why I love it so much."

One of my classmates raised her hand with a concerned look. "I'm pushing the due date for your papers to next Tuesday," said Mr. Mays, without so much as a glance in her direction. She slowly lowered her hand and looked around at her peers, her face visibly blushing even in the faint orange light. The class erupted in muted cheers. Mr. Mays waited patiently for the inevitable silence.

After the remnants of side conversations ceased, Mr. Mays began his story.

I will attempt to recreate how he told his tale to the best of my abilities. It managed to render the horror junkies speechless and the rest of the students terrified. The poor girl who had raised her hand to ask about the paper had her knees glued to her chest by the end of it—a look of terror on her face. Mr. Mays had a way with words I can only aspire to emulate; his speech was rhythmic, entrancing, and very personal. Don't hold me to it.

Mr. Mays and several of his closest friends set out on a cross-country road trip following their graduation. They borrowed a truck from one of their fathers, loaded it with camping gear, and set out to sight-see for the entire summer – their last season of freedom before being forced to face the full extent of responsibilities that come with adult life. The group started outside of the Poconos in New Jersey and drove down to the coast of Florida, over to New Orleans, along the southern border to California, and straight up through the thick forests of Washington and Oregon. From there, they traveled to the Rocky Mountains in Colorado and eventually returned to New York. The idea of unprecedented freedom was intoxicating to a class of high school students. Mr. Mays described the lives many of us envisioned living once our stint in public education ended, and we were eating it out of his hand.

Since Mr. Mays' group consisted of free-spirited college graduates without time constraints or much responsibility, they didn't bring a map on their journey. They often just picked a direction and drove, hoping to eventually find a town to crash in or someplace that looked remote enough that they wouldn't be bothered if they just set up tents for a night or two. After spending a week in Colorado, the group had to travel through the heart of the Midwest, which, as Mr. Mays put it, consisted of "miles and miles of corn, plains, and more corn."

They were somewhere in Nebraska when they decided to pool their remaining cash and stay in a motel for one last night of decent rest before they made the final push toward home. They settled into a rundown inn located in a town that Mr. Mays could barely remember the name of when one of his friends saw a familiar pamphlet for a local fair at the front desk and realized that they were likely somewhere close to a farm that his grandfather owned and that he had visited as a child. After considering the extra beer money they could save if they didn't have to spend it on a motel room, the group decided to hedge their bets and contact the friend's grandpa.

Mr. Mays' friend was unable to reach him on the phone but figured that it would be fine if they just showed up; he was family, after all. The friend was adamant that his grandparents would take them in and feed them without hesitation. So, the group set out with a little over an hour of sunlight left to light their way and sought the salvation of what sounded like a comfortable place to crash.

For those who have never visited, Nebraska isn't exactly known for natural markers that make it easy for lost travelers to find their way; any directions given to someone who isn't familiar with the area basically amount to something like: "Go up a couple of miles to the corn and take a right down a dirt road to the other corn; there should be some wheat on your right." So, as is the case in commonplace stories like this, the group got lost. Refusing to admit defeat, the group drove deep into the night – pulling wrong turns every five minutes – until they found themselves on a dirt road that led to a small, dense forest in the middle of a mostly barren landscape. Whether it was actually the place he thought it to be or whether he was just exhausted and was looking for an excuse to call it a night, Mr. Mays' friend pointed them in that direction, claiming that it was most definitely where his grandparents lived.

Mr. Mays described the road as a "dark path to hell." I wasn't sure how accurate this bit of the story was then because he got overly animated and hyperbolic with his explanations of the *trees that almost tried to grab the car* and the *red eyes* of *countless animals looking at them from the darkness*. Regardless, these horror tropes worked on most of the class; everyone seemed to be anxiously teetering on the edges of their desks.

The group of friends drove on the dark and winding road for fifteen minutes before they came to a clearing that housed a small building and a large grain silo. From the look on his friend's face, Mr. Mays could tell that this guy's grandparents did not live there. But, there was light coming from inside the building, so they figured that, at the very least, the people who lived there could help them find where exactly they were. They were banking on their understanding of small-town hospitality and praying that they wouldn't get shot on sight for trespassing. They pulled the car up near the building. The closer they got to the structure, the more it became apparent that it was less of a home and more of a storage facility. It seemed like somewhere a farmer might keep large tractors or entire herds of animals. Still, the lights were on, so they figured they would try the place.

They approached the building as a group—peeking through the semi-open metal monstrosity of a door to find one large, empty room. Hanging fluorescent lights lit the interior like it was noon, yet the boys couldn't find a soul. At this point, one of Mr. Mays' other friends became convinced that he had seen someone duck into the building as they pulled up. Humoring him, they went inside to see if they could find a hidden office or anything to indicate that people were or had recently been there. Keeping an empty warehouse so extensively lit for no apparent reason seemed ridiculous – someone had to be around.

They found nothing but echoes from their own voices inside, so the group started to roam around the exterior of the property, eventually meandering over near the grain silo. As they got closer, one of them spotted what appeared to be a cellar door hidden on the far side of the structure, obscured by brush.

At this point, I remember Mr. Mays encouraging the class to learn from his idiocy. He told us that he wasn't a fan of horror movies, so he didn't have the typical hang-ups one normally might when approaching creepy cellar doors in the middle of nowhere on dark summer nights. He told us that approaching that door was one of his biggest regrets. For a few moments, he trailed off, almost lost in his thoughts, before regaining himself and diving back into his memories. He said that he felt we were mature enough to handle the part of the story that he was about to get into but advised anyone who was squeamish to leave class early. Several students quietly gathered their things and walked out the door— a couple of them being stoners who saw this as an opportunity to smoke behind the school before their next class. I didn't even give the announcement a second thought; I was a sucker for this kind of stuff. Mr. Mays was telling a story better than anything I had ever conjured up, and I just wanted to take in as much as I possibly could from it.

I wanted to learn from him.

After the class had thinned and quieted once more, Mr. Mays continued. He told the remaining students that he and his friends opened that cellar door—releasing a smell he described as "the most putrid thing my senses have ever experienced." At this point, the group was no longer concerned with finding the property owners but was now set on finding the source of that smell. They went down the steps into the cellar, lit by single bulbs spaced sporadically along the ceiling of a long hallway. No one spoke a word during this time; things had gotten too strange to joke about. The walls were covered with metal sheeting, similar to farm roofing. The structure itself was crooked—ceilings constantly rising and descending like a tunnel that was hastily dug, proceeded to collapse, and was never properly repaired. There were sections where the boys had to crouch to pass. The architecture and layout didn't make much sense, leaving them disoriented – some even felt nauseous.

To add to the effect, the light bulbs along the tunnel continuously flickered like strobe lights, making it very difficult to navigate the winding and ever-changing corridor. Mr. Mays told us that he was sure the lights caused his mind to play tricks on him. He repeatedly caught flashes of objects or people that phased in and out of existence with each bright pulse and couldn't have been there. He said that when you're that focused on something—or if you are anxious enough—your mind can revolt and distort your reality without you even realizing what is happening. He paused for a moment before addressing us very directly.

"What do you do when you can't trust your senses?"

He let us sit with that question for a second before he continued describing the tunnel. I was practically there with him. I could see the winding hallways that seemed to go on forever. I could smell the stench that lingered in the tunnels. I could almost feel the warmth of the glowing bulbs on the walls. Every word brought me deeper into his terrifying world.

At that point, Mr. Mays guessed they were directly underneath the creepy forest they had driven through. Around a slight bend and a low-hanging part of the ceiling, they came upon a door. It was so out of place that even listening to the details was jarring. The door was wooden and relatively modern looking—something suited for the entrance of a suburban home in Anytown, USA. It had an intricate floral design, fresh red paint, and a sumptuous knob and knocker. It made the group uncomfortable. Mr. Mays noted that the floral pattern started from each corner of the entryway and converged in the center, obscuring what appeared to be a large tree with the subtle features of an emaciated face hidden near the base of it. It was so entirely *wrong* – not something you would expect to be sitting in a dirt tunnel in the middle of nowhere. One of Mr. Mays' friends walked towards the door, moving carefully and using one hand to ground him against the increasingly unstable walls surrounding him. He turned to the group and tried to lighten the mood with a laugh before saying, "Should I knock first?"

With a shrug and a smirk, Mr. Mays' friend grabbed the steel knocker and tapped it against the door mockingly while quietly uttering, "Is anyone home?" The group waited about thirty seconds before the tension began to dissipate. The friend by the door shrugged his shoulders and went to walk back to the group. As he did, the light bulb between them quickly surged and exploded. The boys shielded their eyes and looked back to their lone friend. As he lowered his hands, one of the metal sheets from the makeshift roof collapsed onto his forehead—opening up a massive wound and sending a torrent of blood pouring down the shocked expression on his face. The group stood there in confusion and fear for a moment before their now crimson-coated friend looked towards them and lost consciousness, falling back against the door and knocking it open in the process.

The group rushed through the dim light to their friend—barely noticing the dark room before them. Mr. Mays was the first to make it to his friend's side. He lifted his friend's head into his arms, removed his own jacket, and wrapped it over the gaping wound in an attempt to stop the bleeding. Once the collective pulse of the group had slowed, Mr. Mays noticed an ice-cold liquid dripping onto the back of his neck. He was confused and attempting to sort out its source when one of his friends began frantically muttering and retreating back into the tunnels they had just come from. He shrieked something along the lines of, "The lights; we have to go," before fully committing and fleeing the scene entirely.

"You know when you turn off a light, and everything goes *almost* entirely dark, except for the bulb's light dying out or cooling down?" Mr. Mays asked the class. "Well, at least twenty light bulbs had lit the room seconds before that door was knocked open. Now, they just looked like faint stars in the darkness. They gave off just enough light to hint at what awaited us – staring at us from that room. We could make out the silhouettes of what seemed to be tens of people standing just a few feet in front of us. Then, a single bulb to my right came to life with a pop and a hum, lighting the room and leaving no doubt about what stood before us."

Let me interrupt at this point and say that Mr. Mays was a generally playful guy. He had one of those voices that could pull a response right out of you before you could even form the thought yourself. He could say, "Let's jump off a cliff, guys," and you would instinctively ask him to lead the way. His charisma was mesmerizing. He had told the story to this point, like we were all sitting around a campfire. He used his sentences' cadence, inflections, and pacing to build an air of fear and mystery. But, at this point in his tale, I recall his tone changing completely. It seemed like he had stopped trying to scare us. This part of the story appeared difficult for him to remember. It was subtle – so much so that I second-guessed myself as I watched him. Either he was an outstanding actor, and I wasn't as savvy as I thought, or it really was a terrifying memory for him to relive.

He told us how the bulb flickered to life and cast a dim light on the people before him. He could see at least twenty children dressed in nightgowns that were tattered, torn, and stained dark with mud or something worse. Their bodies and faces were nearly obscured by their long and matted-down hair. None of them appeared to have seen a shower or nice bath in their entire life.

Mr. Mays told the class that the most terrifying aspect of the situation was that no child moved an inch. They all stood staring, most only visible from the light reflecting off their eyes. The group was collectively paralyzed with fear when they heard what sounded like an animal in the distance yelping. The sound morphed slowly into something resembling the dying cries of the larger beast – wounded and pleading in the darkness. Despite being unable to determine the full size of the room from the lack of light, he said that the noise filled the space so thoroughly that the creature at the source of the sound would have needed to be impossibly large to conjure such a cry. This spurred the group into desperate action as the children began to step towards them. Mr. Mays' friends grabbed their injured comrade and lifted him out of the room and into the tunnel as quickly as possible.

Mr. Mays took another moment to move and had difficulty finding his bearings. He reached to his left to find a wall to lean against, eventually grasping a handle and pulling on it hard, never taking his eyes off the children.

He was about to bolt for the door when he looked closer at the metal object he had grabbed onto. A showerhead protruded straight out of a bare cement wall about a foot into the room. A viscous brown liquid leaked from the pores, but it was too dim to tell what it might have been. The children stumbled towards him as the creature cried in the distance. He brought himself to his senses and began to move with purpose. Exiting the room, he could make out several more showerheads on the wall near the dim bulb.

"This is why I call them *The Showers*," Mr. Mays told the class.

I could hardly breathe. I was sitting as far forward as my desk would allow, my pulse racing as I braced for more.

"I slammed the red door behind me, catching a glimpse of that floral pattern in the wood one more time," he said. "Then, I ran through those tunnels faster than I had ever run before. I returned to the car, and we drove off like bats out of hell." A couple of students snickered and quietly echoed "hell" to each other. I blinked and was abruptly pulled back to that classroom – back to reality.

"I guess my point is that when you're out *trick-r-treating* tonight, ladies and gentlemen," he said, "make sure that you know exactly where you are headed, and don't go out to any abandoned farmhouses. There aren't many around here, but I think you catch my drift. I'm talking about metaphorical abandoned farmhouses."

The class collectively half-laughed and monotonously said, "Yes, Mr. Mays," as the bell rang for the passing period.

Mr. Mays turned the light on and thanked everyone for listening, reminding them about the paper due the following week. He told us to have a safe and Happy Halloween as the class poured into the hallways, whispering at each other excitedly. Students around me were abuzz with theories about the story they had just heard.

"I bet it was some sort of crazy Nazi hideout," said one girl.

"I think they were all ghosts of kids that were killed by a bear or something," said another.

I was still caught up in the moment—in the story. The way Mr. Mays had weaved that narrative had blown me away. But the detail he included in it, followed by the abrupt ending, left me feeling like we didn't get the *whole* story. I felt that I couldn't move on with my life without closure.

So, a couple of days later, I decided to stay after class and ask Mr. Mays how his story ended, emphasizing his injured friend's uncertain fate. He laughed and assured me that his friend was fine and that the whole mess was "probably due to some of the drugs they were on at the time." I mostly bought his explanation and gave a little chuckle while doing my best to ignore the brief look of genuine fear I was sure I caught in his eyes when I had asked the initial question. He gave me a pat on the shoulder and winked at me as if to say, "Don't tell anyone about the drugs bit, kid." I smiled, left his classroom, and eventually let the lingering uncertainty about the situation fade.

I lived in that town for another couple of months before returning home one day to find a massive U-Haul truck in my driveway—a familiar sight. This time, we were moving halfway across the country to Milwaukee, Wisconsin, so that my mother could take over a managerial position at a major brewing company.

I brought *The Showers* with me wherever I went through the following few years. I twisted the story's details around and told it whenever I could. It was always a hit. I did, however, change the ending from time to time—letting the friend die of blood loss or having the children drag him to his doom. I wanted to give it that last little *punch* I desperately craved when I first heard the story. It became my signature bit – my tribute in spoken word to a teacher who changed my entire approach to storytelling.

It wasn't until college that I got the chance to speak to Mr. Mays again.

I went to University in New York – Ithaca, to be more precise. All in all, I enjoyed school; I continued to be the same ham that I had always been and kept a steady group of a few close friends. It was, without a doubt, the most stable period I had experienced up to that point in my life; I had never spent such a long stretch of time in a single place before that. I felt less restless, allowed myself to form deeper bonds with the people around me, and even had a steady girlfriend for a few years.

At the tail end of my junior year, I ran into Mr. Mays at a bar I frequented near Cayuga Heights.

Initially, I wasn't entirely sure that the guy I saw with his head buried in his arm at the bar was Mr. Mays. It had been years since I had seen him outside of my memories. The dead giveaway was the sweater he had on. He wore it every year on his birthday, so there was no uncertainty; it simply read: "I'm the birthday boy!" A complete lack of subtlety was one of his favorite bits.

I told my friends to grab a table for themselves, and I would join them in a second. I then somewhat cautiously shuffled over to the bar. I cleared my throat before I spoke.

"Mr. Mays?" I said. He slowly raised his head from his arm as if he had an immense weight on him. He studied my face for several seconds with a confused look before a familiar smile crawled across his face. He put a hand on my shoulder and gave me a light shake.

"Hey there, son! How've you been?" he asked. I could smell whiskey on his breath. The look in his eyes and the deep red of his cheeks told me he was three sheets to the wind and probably had no idea who I was. But, he was still the same Mr. Mays – never wanting to make anyone around him less than comfortable. So, he played it off like we were old friends.

"Mr. Mays, my name is Jack," I said, awkwardly attempting to clarify my identity without making him feel bad for forgetting me. "I was a student of yours for a couple semesters about six or so years ago," He looked me over a second time before his face brightened, his shoulders relaxed, and a genuine look of recognition set in.

He nodded, took on a more casual tone, and asked, "How've you been, Jack?"

We talked for what must have been a couple of hours. I told Mr. Mays what I had been up to for the previous several years, and he caught me up on his life in the same way. He was still teaching at the same school and doing "the same old shtick," as he called it. I asked if everything was going well otherwise, and he said they were as good as they had ever been or were ever going to get.

It took a little while for the realization to set in that I was an adult having a conversation with another adult in that bar. When I had spoken to Mr. Mays prior to that night, I had been his pupil, and he had been my teacher—my superior. Now, the dynamic had balanced. I was just a guy drinking with a friend at the bar.

My school friends eventually left while I continued to drink with Mr. Mays. He told me all about his divorce and his kids -- things that I never would have asked or cared about previously. Now, I felt something more. He had become a real person to me – not just an idol or a superior. He was a guy who had real problems—not the infallible master storyteller that I had built him up to be in my head.

I was several drinks deep before I brought up *The Showers*. I had told him about my history with urban legends and scary stories, and he got a real kick out of it. He said that he had always seen that "sparkle" in my eyes, which led him to believe that I would end up telling stories in some form or another. He began to look slightly uncomfortable when I mentioned the particular story he had told our class so many years ago. He finished his whiskey, signaled for another, and turned to me, suddenly sporting a troubled demeanor.

"Listen, Jack... I don't know why I kept telling that story year... after year." His words were slurred; we were both sufficiently blitzed by that point. "That was what the therapists encouraged me to do. I had to tell people about it to *come to grips* with it or some shit..." He trailed off and took a large swig of his drink.

"Your therapist?" I asked, confused.

Mr. Mays snorted and looked over at me with glassy hazel eyes. "Of course, Jack. You think that something like that wouldn't fuck a person up?"

I was unsure of what he meant but half-smiled to show some empathy. I had only begun to notice the deep and dark bags below his eyes – the slight yellow tint to his hands and fingernails. "But, I mean, you said you were all on drugs or something, right? No one got too badly hurt?" The feeling that I had repressed for so many years – the certainty that Mr. Mays had not told us the whole story – came rushing back instantaneously. My heart beat rapidly as I asked a question I thought I knew the answer to. "You were all okay, weren't you?"

He began blubbering over the next several seconds as tears began flowing down his face. "Of course we weren't, Jack. Why do you think I'm here like this?"

I was puzzled—filled with a thousand questions I wanted to ask him, but I let him continue.

"Tim fuckin', he didn't make it, Jack," he laughed before letting loose another wave of tears. "They just fuckin' took him. I don't even know. Cops told us we were just drunk. That he wandered off and got taken by the wildlife. They didn't know. They didn't see, Jack."

I was stone-faced at this point. Mr. Mays was carrying along like I knew the story, but I didn't. His friend had disappeared or *worse*. I had no idea.

"I wish they'd have found the body, though. Then we could have shown them," he sighed. "That's a bad place, Jack. I don't know anything else to say. It's a bad place."

Mr. Mays continued for a couple of minutes more about his friends and the fun they had before their fateful stop in Nebraska. I let him go on without interruption. I was still processing the entire situation; the booze didn't exactly make it easier. It was only a few minutes later that his cell phone rang. He fumbled for it in his pocket and searched for the button to answer it while holding the screen close to his face.

"Hello, sweetheart," he whispered into the phone. "I'll be out in a second. I l–" he hiccupped, "-love you, baby." The person on the other end hung up, and Mr. Mays got up to leave.

"It's been nice seeing you, Jackie," he said as he raised himself off his stool – using my shoulder for support. "You've got a good head. Try to keep it that way." I smiled at him as he began to walk out of the bar. As he turned his back, my brain ran through a flurry of final thoughts, searching for something reassuring or kind to say to him before he left.

"Mr. Mays!" I yelled after him.

"Yeah, Jack?" he turned back towards me – swaying slightly.

"Where'd you say all that shower business took place?" I asked.

"Where? Broken Bow, Nebraska!" he bellowed across the bar. "Fucking Hell on Earth, if you ask me."

Mr. Mays waved to me and walked out of the bar. He bumped into the wall several times before eventually finding the door.

That was the last time I would ever see Mr. Mays. I'd never be able to tell him the impact he had on my life, or rather, the impact his story had on me. He'd never know about the trip we took after graduation that almost mimicked the one he and his friends had gone on so many years ago. He would never know with certainty that the things he saw in those tunnels in Nebraska were real.

He died about a month later. His liver failed him. His daughter, son, and ex-wife were with him in the hospital room. He got to die around people who cared about him, which is all I can ask for a man like that. I just hoped that he found some semblance of peace before he went.

That is where Mr. Mays' story ended; that is also where my story began. The following is how I came to experience *The Showers* on my own some years later – why I refuse to step foot in the state of Nebraska ever again.

I'll start it when I'm sober.

The memory is clear enough now.

PART II

THE HOLE IN THE GROUND OUTSIDE BROKEN BOW, NEBRASKA

OCTOBER 8TH, 2012

I didn't find out about Mr. Mays' passing until a couple of months after his funeral service. Initially, I planned on reaching out to his family to send my condolences. But it wasn't as if Mr. Mays and I were best friends or even particularly close, so I refrained for fear of an awkward encounter.

I continued through my college career and graduated a year or so after our meeting at the bar. Graduating with English as my major wasn't a mistake, but it also wasn't something that landed me a job immediately following graduation. Instead of jumping right into the hunt for an adult job, I opted for a well-deserved vacation. Fortunately, I saved a decent amount of money while in school by working closing shifts at the local independent movie theatre. So, I gathered my spare cash, got together with my college buddy Steve, packed up, and hit the road—aiming for somewhere in the Rocky Mountains. When I was younger, I lived near Littleton, Colorado, and I remember loving the area. Hence, the Rockies were as good a destination as any.

Within a week, we made it to Estes Park, Colorado, and found a cheap cabin that we rented for a month. Our days were filled with lounging, hiking, cards, beer, and fire pits. Our only interactions with civilization came from gas stations, grocery stores, and the local Irish pub that we frequented—Lonigans Saloon.

Sometime during the trip, we met up with a couple of Estes Park natives at Lonigans who were about our age and, luckily, shared a similar love of liquor. We never intentionally *hung out*; we just had conversations now and then over drinks and food when we found ourselves at the bar at the same time, which happened pretty frequently.

One night, these guys were paying their tab and packing up to leave unusually early; it wasn't infrequent for us to close the pub with them. When we questioned them about it, they told us they were headed to a get-together with their friends and proceeded to invite us. Having little else to do, we hopped in the car and followed them to the party.

The party itself was very low-key and ultimately inconsequential to this story. The one important thing about it was that we all wound up sitting around a fire and swapping scary stories at some point in the night. At that point in my life, I didn't have the *need* to be the constant center of attention that I might have possessed in my younger years. But with a bit of coaxing from Steve, I started on a couple of stories I remembered telling in my youth.

Inevitably, I made it to Mr. Mays' story about *The Showers*. Every time I told the story after hearing it for the first time, I tried to "spice it up." But, out of some sort of subconscious respect for my former teacher (or just due to lack of practice), I went straight into the original version that he told my class in my sophomore year of high school. It was like hearing a song from my childhood on the radio; once I hit those first few beats, the rest of the story followed without even having to think about it.

The group enjoyed my stories for the most part, with *The Showers* being the mutual favorite among the partygoers. We played some drinking games, during which I benefitted from my newfound popularity (read: everyone made me drink). I sobered up with some coffee, and we decided to head on our way before the sun started to rise.

Steve and I left for our cabin at around five in the morning. During the drive back, he grilled me about *The Showers* and, being significantly less than sober and still buzzing off of all the attention from the party, I indulged his curiosity. I told him about Mr. Mays, his class, and my love for everything horror-related. Steve suggested we try to find the place for ourselves during our trip back to New York. Initially, I was reluctant simply because I didn't feel like aimlessly wandering through Nebraska for days looking for an old farm building—one that had probably been demolished by that point. But, after a couple of days of persistence on Steve's part, I caved. We wouldn't be able to do another trip like that for a long time – if ever – so I figured that we might as well make the best of it. I was being dishonest with myself at the time, trying to convince myself I wasn't interested in finding the place, however unlikely it may have been. My curiosity was piqued.

We left Colorado and made the long, dull, and barren drive to Broken Bow, Nebraska, or "Hell on Earth," as Mr. Mays had so bluntly put it years before. We found a motel in town and hung around for a couple of days, venturing out a hundred miles or so in any given direction each day after that, blowing through binders of burned CDs that we had listened to countless times by that point. I remembered Mr. Mays telling us that it was somewhere outside of Broken Bow. Still, I don't think he went into any more detail on the location, which meant we used the last of our gas cash fairly quickly.

We asked several townsfolk if they had any information about *The Showers*. When we told them what the place was supposed to be, we were mostly met with blank stares or rolling eyes.

The only person who seemed to know anything about it was an elderly lady who worked at a gas station on the outskirts of town. She was one of those simple, cheerful old people—very helpful, happy to still be alive, and seemingly genuinely interested in any topic of conversation that her customers brought up. I overheard part of a conversation she was having with a group of girls from Oregon wherein she mentioned how her family roots ran deep through Broken Bow. Steve also caught that detail, and we both assumed she would be one of the best bets in our search for more information on *The Showers*. While checking out, he started talking to the old woman about nothing in particular. She asked him about our license plate before commenting that we were far from home. He walked her through the broad beats of our trip and talked to her for about fifteen minutes. At that point, he felt comfortable enough to bring up our real purpose for being in town. I had moved next to Steve by this point, ready to clarify any details from the story to help jog her memory.

Initially, the name didn't appear to ring any bells with the woman, which made sense, considering Mr. Mays told us that he had just called it that because of the showerheads in his story. But, when I began to describe more specific details about the surrounding woods and the farmhouse above the tunnels, the friendly old woman locked eyes with me and interrupted. Her tone was not scornful or mean, but she instantly became terse and deliberate with the following words.

"People don't deal with anything related to that sort of business around here anymore," she told us. That was all a long time ago." There was a pause as Steve and I tried to figure out what we could say to break the sudden tension. After a few moments, her cheerful demeanor returned, and she excused herself to the restroom while wishing us the best on our return trip to New York.

Steve and I walked back to the car in silence and mutual confusion. We were thinking over what the lady had told us *and how* she said it. She didn't seem angry or want to hear another word about it. I can only speak for myself, but at the time, I couldn't stop thinking about how we had stumbled into some sort of situation straight out of *The Wicker Man* or (more appropriately) *Children of the Corn*. Eventually, Steve broke the uneasy silence.

"I mean, if I had to live in a place associated with an urban legend, I would mess with anyone who brought it up," he said. Eventually, you'd just get tired of people asking, and so you'd just try to scare them to shut them up, wouldn't you?" I quietly agreed with Steve, and he kept driving.

But, the experience wasn't sitting right with me. If *The Showers* were a well-known legend in the area, why did no one else in town try to screw with us or scare us off the scent? Why was a little old lady the only person who had shown any semblance of familiarity with our description? We weren't afraid of finding *The Showers*. The little excursion on our road trip was just a bonus—a cap-off to an overall relaxing vacation. If we had gone back home empty-handed, we would have lost nothing but some gas money. Hell, the interaction with the old woman was new material for the next time I told the story, which was a net positive as far as I was concerned.

We decided to spend one more day around Broken Bow before we left for home. Despite wanting to "make it count," we didn't end up leaving the hotel until around noon, thanks to a long and humid sleepless night. When we finally got back on the road, we decided to attempt to stay off the highways for as much of the day as possible. There was no chance the place would be off a main road, so we spent most of our time four-wheeling down dirt roads in what felt like the middle of nowhere. We took any path that seemed *out of the way* or in the least bit *spooky*; any old farming equipment or barns that we could spot instantly became headings. Unfortunately, Nebraska has a surplus of creepy roads, old barns, and rusted-out tractors. After another day with nothing to show for our efforts, Steve and I were ready to leave the state and never look back. But, we had wandered so far into the boonies that our trip back to the hotel was looking to take us deep into the evening.

It was about seven when we came upon a small but dense patch of forest. I use the term lightly, but the place was like an oasis for Nebraska. We had either driven right by it earlier in the day or (and this was an idea that neither of us dared voice) we were *lost*. The trees were full and thick— shrouding most of the interior with darkness. I couldn't figure out how we could have missed it. The sun was setting, and even though we had run into a few of these random crops of trees during the day, we believed we had found one that showed more promise than any others. I figured that even if we *were* lost, we might as well follow up on one more potentially good lead. There wasn't a road but a path where one might have existed at some point, so we followed that. If the car could handle the Rocky Mountains, it didn't seem that a dirt path in Nebraska would give us much trouble.

We took it slowly along the trail, clearing any fallen trees or rocks that would render the car useless. We were spiraling into the thick brush when the sun finished setting. It was dark in that place at twilight, but it became something else entirely when night set in. A feeling of familiarity with a place where I had never been growing in my gut. I didn't want to jinx us, so I stayed silent. The little bits of light penetrating the canopy in the miniature forest made it look like the tree branches were trying to grab the car—just like Mr. Mays had described in his story. There were, however, no animal eyes staring at us from the dark. In fact, the most aggressive creature we spotted was a dead rabbit on the side of the trail—looking like it had simply laid down and never bothered to get up.

We drove around in the darkness for quite a while before we found an entrance to the clearing. We had to move several small clusters of branches out of our way before discovering our biggest hurdle yet. Right in front of our entrance sat the carcass of a gigantic tree. It looked as if it had been plucked from the redwood forests of California and dropped amongst a pile of twigs; it was at least three times the diameter of anything else in that place – the car included. There was simply no way that we would be able to move it. Steve angled the car so that the high beams pointed into the clearing as I got out and walked around the massive, rotting monstrosity. I felt simultaneous excitement and dread when I saw what sat fifty yards beyond our roadblock.

There, partially lit by the headlights and the pale glow from a mostly full moon, was an old farmhouse. It didn't seem to be a typical farmhouse. It was much larger than the barns I had seen in films and didn't have any sort of crest. It looked more like a small warehouse than anything. I wasn't entirely sure at this point if it was the place we were looking for, but it was definitely the closest we had come.

I moved through the clearing until I was roughly twenty feet from the entrance to the structure, at which point all of the foliage

I had been moving through came to an abrupt end. I don't know what the owners had done to the soil, but the entire building had a clean-cut border that was clear of any sort of plant life – or any signs of life at all. Cautiously, I approached the entrance—a large sliding door—as Steve came up behind me with two flashlights in hand.

"So you were just going to run off into that place in the dark?" he laughed.

I chuckled half-heartedly and grabbed one of the lights from his hand. Mine was a small but decently bright flashlight – the kind a hiker might fasten to their backpack.

Holding the flashlight in my mouth, I grabbed the metal door with both hands and gave it a tug. It moved slightly and creaked slightly but was too heavy for me to move alone. Steve came up from behind me, set his flashlight on the ground, and grabbed the side of the door.

"One, two… three!" we screamed. I pulled at the door with all that I could muster. We managed to move it a couple of inches when I felt a click – it had fixed back onto its track. From there, it began to roll with ease. With a loud thud that echoed through the open darkness, it stopped. Steve picked up his flashlight and walked behind me; I had already moved inside.

The interior of the building was exceptionally bare. The absence of any trace of life was troubling. There were no broken beer bottles or empty bags of chips; there weren't any animal droppings or eager plants growing there; there wasn't even any graffiti – inside or outside. Only a fine cloud of dust seemed motionless as it hung in the air around us. The room was expansive and more extensive than the average farm, I guessed. Though, it wasn't the warehouse-sized monstrosity that Mr. Mays described in his story. At that point, I convinced myself that it was likely just a random storage area for farming equipment. Considering the remote nature of its location and lack of easy access, it seemed like somewhere better suited for something secret and sinister rather than productive. But, whatever purpose it may have served at one point, it looked like a massive disappointment to me at that moment.

I wandered near the entrance while Steve ventured into the expanse of darkness. As I ran over the story in my mind again, one particular detail struck me like lightning: There was supposed to be a grain silo near the farmhouse. I ran outside and scanned the property as I circled the perimeter of the building. Obviously, a silo isn't difficult to spot, but if one ever sat near that structure, there *had* to be some sort of evidence of its existence. Despite my hopes and efforts, I found only dirt and empty space that stretched from the building to the tree line.

I walked back into the building, frustrated and tired. Steve was still excited—eagerly running around and searching every inch of the place with his light.

"If I could just find one of the showerheads, we would know for sure," he said. "We just need *something* to show for all of this. Just keep looking with me for a little longer." I didn't want to kill his excitement. I had told Steve the story several times, but he didn't know it well enough to realize that place didn't quite match Mr. Mays' description. The building was most definitely an oddity; it was out of place and oddly pristine, but it wasn't the location of *The Showers*. I let Steve explore for a bit longer before calling him over.

"This is probably as close as we're going to get," I said. "But it isn't our place." Remember the silo?" His face went from excitement to disappointment instantly, like a young child who had just opened a pair of socks on Christmas morning. I gave him a sympathetic pat on the shoulder, "It is still a pretty cool spot, though. We could still *tell* people that we found it." I shot him a wink and a cheeky grin. Steve laughed.

"Yeah, man, I guess we could. It's definitely creepy enough," he said. "We should get some pictures as *proof,* you know?" I nodded in agreement. "I'm going to grab the camera real' quick." Steve bolted out the entrance of the building, leaving me alone.

The air was still inside the structure. I could hear the faint sound of Steve running through the brush to the car, but it quickly faded. The room fell utterly silent. I couldn't hear wind or so much as a chirping cricket as I walked deeper into the dark, flashlight in hand. As I moved, an uncomfortable feeling tugged at me. Even if that wasn't *The Showers*, something about the whole place just felt wrong. The location, the inexplicable cleanliness, and the fact that such a large structure was hidden so far away from society in an area so difficult to access – it didn't add up.

I approached the far corner of the room – still searching for anything to help me make sense of it all. A soft, hollow thud interrupted the rhythmic sound of my feet scratching against the dirt. I stopped, puzzled, and again hit my foot against the ground. Another *thud* echoed beneath me.

I walked to the nearby wall and looked carefully over the floor to try and spot any holes or gaps. As far as I knew, there was nothing but solid ground below me. I was convinced that I had found a hatch or the entrance to a basement. *Showers* or not, it appeared to me that we had at least discovered something of interest. I was buzzing with cautious excitement when I heard Steve moving through the brush on his return to the building.

"Steve!" I shouted. "Come over here! The ground is hol-"

As I went to speak the word "hollow," I hopped a little bit—hoping to recreate the sound so that Steve could hear it. The instant my feet made contact with the floor, it gave way beneath me.

My memory of the fall is fuzzy, but I recall hearing wood splinter. I remember seeing the light from Steve's flashlight disappear as I slipped into darkness. It wasn't a long fall – no more than twelve feet, I imagine – but I landed so my legs buckled. My head smacked something solid before hitting the ground. I lost consciousness for several seconds, at least.

When I came to, I was staring into a bright halo of light. For an instant, I thought that I was approaching the fabled light at the end of the tunnel. I felt angry with myself. *You died in Nebraska, Jack? You really do know how to fuck up.* But my apparent heavenly ascension was interrupted by Steve's voice. I should have known I wouldn't be headed upward in the end, anyway.

"Jesus, Jack! Jack, can you hear me?" he screamed. "Wake up. Move! Please, wake up!"

I managed to lift my head up off of the floor just enough to ease his concerns. I knew that I had a concussion instantly, but that thought was drowned out by a searing pain shooting through my knee. I fumbled until my hand found my little flashlight hiding just a few feet away from me under a couple of pieces of splintered wood. I proceeded to sit up and reassure Steve.

"I'm alive! I think I just hurt my knee. I bumped my head too – fucking hard," I said. His light was making my head hurt worse. "Can you stop shining that thing in my face?" He apologized and pointed it up towards himself.

"Thank fuck, man. I thought you were dead," he said. "Imagine that – you dying in fucking *Nebraska* of all places." This caused me to chuckle, which I immediately regretted when the slight motion in my neck sent pulsing pain through my temples and caused my vision to blur. The slightest shaking stung my head and made me dizzy.

"I guess, uh… rope?" said Steve.

"What?" I asked, closing my eyes tight.

"Should I get a rope to get you out of here, or do you see a ladder?" I looked at the smooth cement wall in front of me. I couldn't see a ladder, and there was no way in hell I was going to make it up the wall.

"Yeah, get the rope," I told him. "It's buried under a bunch of shit. I think it might be in my red climbing bag, but I'm unsure." Steve nodded, told me he would be back as fast as he could, and then ran off into the night once more.

After the sound of Steve's feet stomping across the floor above me faded, the only thing I could hear was the faint buzzing that only occurred in total silence. It made my stomach clench with anxiety. I carefully pushed myself over to the nearest wall and braced myself against it as gently as possible. I focused on relaxing and taking deep breaths to calm my nerves. The cement was ice cold against my back. I had on only a thin T-shirt because it was a humid eighty or ninety degrees outside. But the room felt like a walk-in meat freezer.

I picked hair anxiously from the goosebumps on my arms while I waited for Steve in what felt increasingly like my tomb. The pain in my head and knee, coupled with the embarrassment from having fallen down there in the first place, kept my mind running and my blood pumping. It all seemed to instantaneously fade into the background when I heard the light sounds of labored breathing coming from my left.

I tried to convince myself that my injured and anxious head was playing tricks on me, but my mind insisted on returning to Mr. Mays' story. When I first heard it in that classroom years before, I felt nothing but excitement at the idea of such a terrifying scenario. I remember excitedly running it over in my head on repeat while trying to figure out how I would respond if I were the one who had been down in those tunnels. But, as I sat in that dark basement in the middle of Nebraska, living out my slowly escalating horror story, I only felt dread. I wanted the adrenaline to leave my body; I wanted my heartbeat to slow; I wanted to be draped in a blanket by a campfire with friends telling terrifying stories – I didn't want to be living one.

I pointed my flashlight toward the source of the sound and exhaled in relief when my light found nothing but the slowly settling cloud of dust that had been kicked up during my fall. I breathed deeply once more before I heard yet another noise somewhere in the darkness around me. It was so sharp and quick that I couldn't be sure it wasn't my own body moving around without me noticing. I held my breath and focused my attention. After several seconds of silence, I caught a very light scraping sound no more than ten feet in front of me. It sounded like bare feet dragging across the dirt just slowly enough that they *might* have gone unnoticed if I hadn't been listening for them. Before I could react, I heard the breathing once more. It was closer that time. My head spun in circles, trying to rationalize the situation. I hadn't seen so much as a spider web in the building above, yet I sat there listening to what sounded like creatures breathing and moving all around me. It didn't make sense. I quickly turned towards another scraping noise, accidentally dropping my flashlight in the process. The room fell once more into darkness.

I grew angry at myself for getting so worked up. I knew that all of it had to be in my head. I told myself repeatedly that the human brain constantly hallucinates. I told myself that while immersed in total silence or darkness, my brain would fabricate sights and sounds to fill the void. My makeshift mantra worked for a few precious moments before I heard the sound of something significant dragging across the floor in front of me. I could listen to the weight of it as it moved across the dirt. It wasn't trying to hide itself any longer. I panicked and desperately searched the space around me for my light.

In a stroke of good fortune, my fingers found the cold metal and gripped it tightly. I struggled for a moment. I wanted to use the light – to prove to myself that there was nothing with me in that basement. But, if there *was* something down there, I would have given myself away entirely by turning it on. I stuffed the light securely in my jeans pocket. *If I couldn't see it, then it couldn't see me.*

I quietly pushed back against the cold cement wall in an attempt to stand. I somehow managed to get up on one foot despite my anxious shaking and busted knee. I felt up and down my leg with my free hand. There was blood – I could smell it in the air before I felt it in my drenched denim pants. A piece of my jeans had been ripped clean off in the fall and had taken quite a bit of flesh with it. I limped along the wall, eventually finding a corner to settle in momentarily. I quietly hummed to myself – only loud enough for me to hear – in a small attempt to ward off the suffocating silence. I tried my best to call for Steve but struggled with paralyzed vocal cords and what felt like a layer of dust coating my throat. A pathetic whimper was the best that I could manage. I figured he was still in the back of the car, hunting for the rope. For the time being, it was me versus the darkness, and my own head wasn't on my side.

At that point, I made a choice to find my own way out. I was under a building, meaning the place had to have stairs or a ladder somewhere. Either option sounded a hell of a lot easier than climbing a rope in my injured state. Even if I was stuck in a labyrinth, I would eventually be able to find my way out if I stuck to one wall.

My heart, which had been beating out of my chest, slowed to a manageable rate as I hummed and moved through the dark—keeping my whole body against the wall and as much weight off of my injured leg as possible. I hadn't traveled further than ten feet when my head made contact with a rusty metal bar protruding from the wall. I collapsed onto the ground.

The air left my lungs as I hit the dirt with an involuntary *yelp!* My head thumping and my body painfully pulsing, I brought my hands to my face. A warm and wet liquid ran down my cheeks. Despite my best efforts, I could find no broken skin. I pulled the flashlight from my pocket as I sat up and braced myself against the wall again. I wasn't sure how long the cheap little accessory would hold out, but after that fall, I had to reorient myself. With the light in my right hand and my left hand braced against the wall, I switched on the torch. The floor where I had just fallen was wet, but the dirt had muddled the color of whatever liquid saturated it. I focused my blurred vision on the puddle. *It had to be my blood. What else could possibly-*

I felt like I was dreaming as I watched the tiniest drop of liquid – no larger than a pea – sail in slow motion through my light's beam and land in the puddle with a *plop* that shattered the silence. I knew then *exactly* where it came from, but I tried endlessly to convince myself I was wrong. With trembling hands, I raised the flashlight and pointed it above me. What stared back was a pipe that protruded more than a foot straight out of the concrete wall. The metal was rusted and cracked. Little bits of liquid began to seep from the gaps, giving it a faint glimmer in the light as if it had been sweating. At the end of the pipe was a *showerhead* aimed straight down towards the ground.

I stared in disbelief while my stomach went into a slow-motion free-fall. I tried to ignore the pain in my knee and continued to shuffle along the wall as quickly as I could manage. I could hear a cacophony of noise all around me, but I couldn't be sure they weren't just the sounds of my frantic movement. The other explanations elbowed their way to the front of my mind despite my best efforts to keep them at bay.

I managed to pass under the next showerhead without incident; it was higher than the previous spout and appeared to leak the same nebulous, brown liquid. My path began to feel never-ending – infinite. Every ten feet or so was a showerhead followed by ten more feet of concrete and dirt, followed by another showerhead – rinse and repeat. They began to gush more profusely, but the thick liquid oozed slowly through the pores as if it were being forced out.

A smell not unlike sulfur began to envelop me, making my eyes water and my stomach turn. My mind returned once more to how Mr. Mays had described the putrid stench of that place in his story. I grabbed a handful of my shirt and forced it over my nose. It hardly held back the odor at all. It smelled like vomit; it smelled like shit; it smelled like burnt hair; it smelled like *rot*.

I continued along my path for a few seconds longer before I unexpectedly slid from the wall to the open air and fell. My knee hit the ground hard. The pain was blinding—a harsh white flash stung my retinas like I had just been hit by a camera flash. Despite the fall, I had managed to keep a hold of my flashlight. I aimed it all around, trying to grasp my new surroundings.

Standing before me was a door. It had an aesthetically pleasing floral pattern carved into it, a bronze doorknob, and a simple metal knocker. Though the wood was worn, I could make out what appeared to be an emaciated-looking face at the base of a massive tree – the centerpiece of the pattern, even though it was mostly obscured by flowers. I sat at eye level with it, staring into hollow holes dug in place of my eyes. I could see a glint of something in the dark pits and began to feel uneasy like I was staring at an optical illusion that my brain couldn't quite sort out. I forced my glance away from the face. Red paint peeled from the door, flaking off and falling gently to the ground before me. A deep, rumbling noise from behind me broke my trance.

I rose clumsily and – with a deep breath – burst through the door with my shoulder leading the dead weight of my body. My head narrowly missed a piece of hanging sheet metal before I landed on the ground. I gathered myself and examined the new room. I was at the start of a hallway lined haphazardly with identical, rusty metal sheets. My flashlight reached only a few feet in front of me before being swallowed by a distinctive, inky darkness. Fortunately for my leg, it appeared that I wouldn't need to walk on it in the tunnel. The jagged metal pieces were held up by columns of rotting wood – the only thing that kept the place from caving in on itself. I couldn't risk sliding along those hazards and slicing up my sides or causing the tunnel to collapse. So, I crawled.

I pulled myself along the ground for what felt like miles, running into walls every now and then on a path that curved like a snake. I had no way of telling where I was at any given time in relation to the hole that I had fallen through. The further I moved down that winding corridor, the more I had to keep myself from panicking.

There had to be an exit at the end of it.

As I moved along, I couldn't help but consider the structure of the tunnel around me. There were parts where the ceiling dipped down to only two or three feet above the ground. The place hadn't caved in only because of the pillars and sheet metal, but even the most claustrophobic sections seemed well-covered and surprisingly sturdy despite the ramshackle appearance. I considered briefly why someone would intentionally design the entrance or exit to any location in such a disorienting and dangerous way but stopped before arriving at the potential rationale.

I quickly turned my focus to ignoring the sound of scraping several feet behind me, which seemed to mimic my movements with only the slightest discernable delay.

I ignored the way my jeans brushed against my legs in a way that felt like fingers hovering around them in preparation for a grip.

I *had* to ignore the voices that seemed to hide behind my body's sounds as I dragged along the dirt floor.

I had to ignore these sensations and observations because the alternative – the potential truths – seemed mentally insurmountable.

I continued, heart racing and blood freezing until I felt the Earth beneath me begin to slope upwards. I craned my neck and saw the saving grace of a wooden cellar door. Slivers of light shined through the gaps in the wood and dimly lit the distance between salvation and me. *The headlights—it had to be the headlights from our car*—meant that warmth and safety were only just beyond that door.

When I finally reached the door, I slammed my shoulder against the wood without hesitation. It budged, but only slightly. I pushed my back and shoulders against it while inhaling a dust cloud. My throat seared with pain as I attempted to yell out for Steve. The only sound I could emit was like the noise air makes when forced through a broken recorder, with occasional instances of a high-pitched cry. Frustrated and exhausted, I relaxed and let my body rest awkwardly between the ground, the door, and the rusty metal on the wall. I could feel the sharp edges as they ran against my skin, leaving small incisions along their paths. I couldn't find the energy to care. My eyes rested, staring upwards at the slits of light before me. Freedom felt so close.

In that moment of silent defeat, I heard a noise that was undoubtedly something moving around in the tunnel. I forced myself to turn around and leaned hard against the cellar door. The sound was slow, deliberate. It started with one long, exaggerated shuffle, paused momentarily, and repeated. I began to hyperventilate. It was getting closer. I was panicking; I had to do something. I took one deep breath and held it in as I aimed the flashlight's beam into the tunnel.

What I saw in the light, I still struggle to rationalize.

Before me stood a child in a dirty sleeping gown—stained dark brown with scattered splashes of a deep red. Its body was withered and frail, like that of a victim from a Holocaust concentration camp. For just a moment, I could make out one of its bloodshot eyes in the beam of my light. When I caught the faint glimmer in the dark, the child shifted and twitched violently. Its eye retreated behind tufts of long, matted hair that reached far beyond its dirt-caked fingertips. The boy, or girl—I'm not entirely sure which—moved towards me with difficulty. It wasn't breathing hard, but every movement was labored. Even beneath the nightgown, I could see its muscles shake and strain under the weight of its skeletal frame.

I would have wanted to help if not for what I had seen in the child's eye. That quick glimpse evoked anger and a burning, deep-seated hatred. With every sharp breath and every arduous step, I could better grasp its intention—one it would see to with every last ounce of energy it had. It meant me *harm*, and—hallucination or not—it was inching closer.

Tears began welling in my eyes, but I couldn't stop staring at it. The goosebumps all over my body felt like needles. I refused to turn off my light. My lungs burned, but I couldn't catch a deep enough breath to ease the pain amid my panic. *I refused to die in the dark.* The child was almost at my feet. I pushed up against the cellar door with everything I had in one last desperate attempt at escape; it somehow felt heavier than before. My final push did nothing, and my body relaxed, resigning itself to whatever fate the child had in store for me, when I heard a voice emanate from behind the wooden door.

"Hey, Jack," it whispered through the gaps in the boards. *It had to be Steve.*

I tried replying – fully intending on saying, "Open this up and get me the fuck out of here right now." But given my shock, all that came out was a pathetic and unintelligible mumble. I clawed at the door—pushing against it with renewed purpose – tearing skin and losing entire fingernails in the process. Finally, I broke eye contact with the child. As I did, the flashlight fell from my lap. It turned off as it hit the ground and rolled down the slope into the tunnel.

"What do you see?" the voice whispered with a tone of simultaneous curiosity and apathy.

"What the *fuck* are you talking about?" I cried, closing my eyes.

"Just take a look, Jack. Tell me what you see," the voice replied calmly. My screams of frustration began to drown out the words. I was mumbling like a maniac when I heard it speak once more, a hint of frustration in its voice. "Just rest for a second. I've got you."

The statement took a second to set in, and I closed my eyes even tighter while reluctantly easing off the door.

"Steve, just do it, please. Just get it open, please," I whimpered. "Just get me *out* of here." My voice grew louder with each passing second. "Steve, you open this *fucking* door right fucking now!"

I opened my eyes briefly and saw nothing but thick strands of black hair dangling before me. A tiny glint of yellow was nearly obscured in the tangled mess but found a way to shine through. There was so much darkness in that little bit of light. I slammed my eyes shut once more and screamed until it felt like my throat was tearing itself apart.

"*Open the fucking–*"

The space behind me turned to open-air almost instantaneously, and I fell back onto the dirt outside. The warm humidity of the clearing felt like a blanket to my lungs, but I knew I couldn't rest just yet. My eyes remained closed as I scrambled for the cellar door behind me. I found a handle and lifted the pallet-sized monstrosity up and over, letting its weight carry it back down against the dirt with a resounding *thud*. I sat back and caught my breath as I slowly let my eyes relax and open.

The barn stood in front of me—illuminated by a car's headlights. My head pulsed with pain. My knee was, at best, dislocated. I was covered in a mix of filth that I didn't want to think about. But despite all of that, I was out of the tunnel. I took another deep breath and buried my head in my hands.

"Steve, why didn't you just fucking open the door?" I waited for a response, but none came. I was shaking and crying; I was angry. I erupted in a mess of frustration and fear. "I was fucking *clawing – screaming* for my life, and you felt like *screwing around* with me?" Still, I heard nothing. I slowly turned and stared in disbelief at the space behind me. Only a large mass of brush led up to the tree line. I couldn't quite figure out what was happening, but I was still heated. "Steve, this is not the fucking time," I said, annoyed. "Come out of the fucking bushes!"

A light breeze swept through the clearing, causing the bush and trees to sway. It carried with it a voice—a faint, desperate yell from the direction of the farmhouse. A lone flashlight bobbed up and down in the dark. I watched as, in the distance, Steve ran into the open door of the structure, screaming my name. He had a purple climbing rope hung over his shoulder.

I lost consciousness at that point. Steve stood over me when I awoke, desperately trying to wake me. I could hear his words but had difficulty processing them. I just looked around and tried my best to piece everything together.

Steve helped me to my feet and walked me to the car. As we pulled away from the scene, I looked back one last time, dazed. My illuminated flashlight sat just outside the cellar door. After a few seconds, the light died, and the clearing was again dark.

Steve drove me straight to the nearest hospital. I don't remember much, but he told me he drove around for an hour before finding anything resembling a main road.

I never told Steve the entire story from my point of view. He probably thought I just knocked myself crazy in the fall and never really asked about it.

—⟋⟍—

After we returned to the East Coast, the two of us drifted apart. He got a new job; I got a new apartment. There was no intention behind it, but we just eventually faded from each other's lives like people tend to do.

As far as what happened to me that night, I have never been able to fully wrap my head around it. Most of it can be semi-rationalized if I can convince myself that I had a nasty concussion. I could have hallucinated many things down in those tunnels, but that doesn't explain everything. I'm not even entirely sure where to draw the line between what was real and what was a product of my imagination.

The tunnel, the door, and the showerheads were real. I can still feel the oily liquid that dripped from them on my skin. To me, these things still fit within the realm of possibility.

The Showers, whatever they may be, might have some legitimate, real-world function that I am ignorant of. I might have stumbled in on some old property that I didn't understand and had an accident that led me to scare the shit out of myself. But take, for instance, something like the cellar door. It was locked, and then it wasn't. I tried to flip a locked door that weighed as much as a ton of bricks for what felt like ages until it flew open damn near on its own. Those are the details my head incessantly turns over while I lie awake in bed every night. Sure, I could have played a sick game with myself in my concussed state. But when you try to stretch rationality and skepticism too far, your solutions can sound *even crazier* than the alternative.

I am still a skeptic, but I believe in what happened to me at *The Showers*. I'm not a hermit or a recluse because of it. I drink a lot, but I function. My head just gets stuck on it some nights. If the things I heard and saw in those tunnels that night were real, it would have a snowballing effect on my entire perception of reality – of this world and how I've experienced it my whole life. So, I'm still working on the story I tell myself about that night.

The most significant impact on me is that I've developed a complete aversion to revisiting the state of Nebraska. *Showers* or no *Showers*, no one will be able to convince me otherwise. I also don't really watch horror movies much anymore. I guess I lost the desire to chase that feeling of fear after Broken Bow. I got my fill of terror for a lifetime or more.

That's it, really.

There isn't much of an ending to my story, as dull as that might sound. I was changed by my experience, sure. But there's no way to change anything about what happened to me. There isn't anything to *fight back* against. Like I said, I teeter back and forth on what I think was real and what might have been the result of some bruising in my brain. But I'm never going to have those definite answers. You now know as much about that place as I do, for all intents and purposes. So, if you find any definitive answers, I'd love to hear them. Maybe I would rest easier.

Before this story, there wasn't really a way to find information about *The Showers*. The legend didn't extend outside of Mr. Mays' classroom. No one else has told a story like this to keep people away from that place – the knowledge just wasn't out there. I guess that's the point of sharing this if there even needs to be one.

I want you to know from me what this place is like. Maybe it's some twisted, drunken logic – or the kid inside me wanting to spread these kinds of stories like I did when I was younger.

I don't know; I don't care. But this is out there now for people to take as they will.

More importantly, it's finally out of my head.

It's getting late, and I'm getting another drink.

Cheers.

More than five years passed without any comment or follow-up from Jack.

PART III

THE SPIRAL

MARCH 12ᴛʜ, 2018

My name is Jack, and some of you may have read or heard a story about me – by me – a few years ago.

I'm writing this from the same shitty laptop that I used to drunkenly post *The Showers* online a little over five years ago. It has spent the better part of two years at the bottom of a box in my bedroom closet. I haven't had much use for it recently, and honestly, it isn't in the best shape. The damn thing takes about twenty minutes to start up properly and dies the instant it unplugs from its charger. Some of the keys are missing. Some of them stick. I've spent much time carefully cleaning soft drinks and whiskey from every last nook and cranny. Still, a thing can only take so much abuse before it just dies.

Tonight, I got lucky.

She managed to boot, just for me. I think she has one more decent story left in her, for better or worse.

I don't really remember writing or posting the first two parts of *The Showers*. However, I remember what my life was like around that period. I was simultaneously listless and restless most days. I wasn't working in my chosen field and had too much time to think about that. I told my story to some friends at a bar one random night, which shook loose some memories and led to that post.

One evening, I woke up and hopped on my laptop to find the story posted in a thread I had left open. I had typed it directly into the submission box; I didn't even leave myself any time to edit. I just forced it out of me over several long nights and threw it on the internet for everyone to see. Even though I didn't necessarily want to relive the whole story in excruciating detail, the post was a real task. Each spelling and grammatical error made me want to shoot whiskey or chug bleach. I went with the former, and as far as I can remember, I have never made it through the whole story as it was written. It seems pointless to go back and read it even now. I've lived through the events enough times in my head. There's no need for me to subject myself to that again.

I did read the comments on the story, however. I wasn't exactly overflowing with self-esteem at the time, so seeing interest in my work boosted my confidence, if only for a moment. Now and then, I would go back to check on them, but for the most part, I was forced to continue with my stagnant life while the story spread quietly around the web.

I was a bartender in those days. I mostly split my free time between sleeping and drinking, which often overlapped with work. I had carved a vicious little loop in a very short period of time. I wasn't a writer like I had hoped to be at that point in my life, so getting to play one on the internet helped to break up the monotony of my reality.

Over the several months following my post, I received several emails and friend requests from old classmates or strangers who had taken an interest in *The Showers*. My former classmates' messages generally consisted of their memories of Mr. Mays and his story and asked nothing in return. I guessed most of them were either married or needed a dose of nostalgia as a pick-me-up, so I often indulged them.

Some wanted to meet in person, grab drinks, and *dive* into the past. I lived half a continent away from the town where I attended Mr. Mays' class at this point, but that didn't stop me from making empty offers of company to several different people if our paths were to ever cross. Once, I wound up grabbing a beer with a guy "just passing through" on a summer night in Denver. The meetup wasn't quite what I was expecting. I'm ninety-nine percent sure he had never had Mr. Mays as a teacher or had even met me before that night. He dodged specifics when I asked him questions and mostly repeated my statements in agreement. He nodded his head a lot and said, "Yeah, that's right," over and over again. But he was picking up the tab, so I didn't think about the strangeness of it all until the following afternoon. That was the first *and* last time I met up with anyone from the internet.

I received a surprising number of requests for the specific coordinates of *The Showers* from a handful of truly strange individuals. People offered money, transport, and even what was essentially militia support if I were to take them there—like it was some sort of guided tour. I turned them down, but I would be lying if I said I didn't consider accepting some cash in exchange for the coordinates of any random barn I could pull up on Google Maps.

As foreign and surreal as the whole thing was, I took immediate notice of the pull the story gave me over people. After the post, I felt more comfortable bringing it up in person. Every subsequent retelling made me feel like I was back around a campfire with friends who hung on my every word. It felt *good* to have such a command over people's attention. I often found myself out with friends, searching for some decent conversation or a one-night stand, and would whip the story out like a party trick. Once we had an audience, a friend would inevitably bring up *The Showers* and beg me to tell the story. I would half-heartedly fight them on it before giving in, ordering another round, and launching into some variation of my bit. It worked almost *too* well. Every time I went out, I seemed to end up with either a new friend or another notch on my belt. I hardly had to try. For me, it was just stumbling down memory lane. After a while, I narrowed my sights—only bringing out the story for certain people for very particular ends.

In short, I used it to get laid.

I'd chat with the girl for a little while, get to know her enough to take a guess at some of her fears, and work them into the climax of my story. I faced down ghosts, encountered demons, and even had spiders rain down on me from the showerheads; you name a fear, and I've likely used it in one iteration of the ending or another. But, I managed to make it out of *The Showers* intact every time—if only ever-so-slightly worse for wear. I appeared just damaged enough by the experience that a pretty girl might feel some level of sympathy for me. I'd thank her for her kindness while reaching out for her hands or leg. This series of events always eventually led to the same place: hers.

I'd stumble back to my barren apartment every afternoon, throw on some different clothes, and head back out to the bar for work, play, or both.

It's unclear to me how long I spent living like the sleazy piece of shit that I just described. But, I know that Karen broke me out of the pattern. Initially, she was just the next in a long line of women I had yet to sleep with. We met at a bar. I told her my story. We wound up at her place. But, instead of passing out after sex like I usually tried to do to avoid further conversation, we actually stayed up and talked. To my surprise, the conversations that we had didn't feel like needless, silence-filling bullshit; I felt like she understood me, and I, her. She was an intensely empathetic person, a trait I latched onto. She wanted to walk through the *emotions* involved in what had happened to me instead of just listening to the story. I don't think I was frank about any of that, but I hadn't experienced a reaction like hers after countless times I ran through *The Showers*, so I was caught off guard and almost instantly smitten with her.

In hindsight, I think our initial connection centered chiefly on our mutual interest in getting really messed up and swapping stories about our shitty lives and mental ailments with another person so that we wouldn't have to make excuses for being alone. But it didn't feel like that at the time.

Funny enough, we actually do have the mental stuff in common – two different kinds of Bipolar Disorder. We were "imperfectly complementary," as Karen always put it. We thought that, in some strange way, it meant we were perfect for each other. I don't need to be told how stupid that sounds.

Before I get ahead of myself, let me say this: Karen had a degree in political science from Rutgers, a wicked right hook, and one of the most persuasive and charismatic personalities I have ever encountered. It worries me that truths like those – the little things that made up who she was as a person – aren't going to come across here because of what all this is ultimately leading to. I just don't want to do her a disservice. She's a flesh-and-blood real person, and any number of words I type about her won't paint her as she actually was. You're getting my skewed version of who she was to me at that point in my life. It is nowhere near enough for you to understand who she actually was – to judge her. Suffice it to say, we didn't end up together for two years because we were awful for each other. We had a genuine, *intense* connection that just wore down with time and probably burned out too quickly, as those things tend to do.

At that point in my life, I was both lost and an asshole. Karen fit into a mold or archetype in my head—the Nancy to my Sid, the Bonnie to my Clyde—and at the time, I didn't consider the possibility that we might end up heading down the same path as both of those famously toxically codependent couples. She was my *manic pixie dream girl*, as awful as that was. I was just a lonely guy looking for a girl with hair the color of a mood ring who listened to the same shitty music that I listened to and who could also solve the complex problem that was *me*.

On any given day, she was the love of my life and my partner in crime. The next day, she could be my antagonist—an obstacle in my search for happiness. It was all part of this story I had seen play out in movies and books countless times before. I tried to force myself into it; in the end, it was me trying to fit a square peg in a nonexistent hole.

She made me feel good about myself for a little while, for whatever that's worth. No one person had managed to do that before Karen. I'm pretty sure I loved her; it's just that I was simultaneously loving her and using her without actually realizing what I was doing. That's not to say she didn't get use out of me.

She started coming over to my place after we spent a couple of nights together, and she never really left. Items of her clothing and toiletries began showing up around the apartment, and I just kind of rolled with it. There was one night when I brought up how we had never actually discussed living together before it had already happened; that night ended with both of us yelling and blacking out in tears. But, by the time happy hour rolled around the following evening, we were as good as new, and in the same place, we were before that unpleasantness. The fighting and passive aggression fit the tone of my previously mentioned "vicious loop," so it didn't feel unhealthy, exactly. We just sort of fell into a jagged groove with each other and accepted it as our life together.

I might have gotten a little off track.

Karen took a great interest in my stories. *The Showers* particularly interested her because she had come across a reading of it on a podcast or YouTube channel and knew about it before she had even met me. She initially thought I was messing with her at the bar—trying to take credit for a story someone else had lived. Eventually, I convinced her of the truth, and she didn't let it go. After long nights out, we would lie in bed together, and she would ask me to tell it again like some sort of morbid bedtime story. With each retelling, I would embellish a little more or shake loose a new "memory" pulled from deep within my imagination to keep her on her toes and the story fresh. I don't know if she believed any of it after a while or just wanted to, but it became our "thing." Eventually, the story wasn't enough. She wanted to live it.

"Can we go there?" she asked constantly. "Let's go to *The Showers*."

Karen wanted us to face down *The Showers* like a boss fight in a video game. She constantly reiterated that it would be good for me to return there and get "perspective." She was also convinced that it might help me pick up writing again, something I had neglected or made excuses to avoid throughout our relationship. She often told me I had such good ideas, but something kept me from letting them loose. She genuinely wanted to help, but I wasn't willing to hear her out. I was steadfast in my resolve that I would never return to Nebraska. I was confident that I had moved on from that horrific night entirely – that all I had brought back with me was a scary story. Everything seems so fucking evident in hindsight.

Another aspect of her interest in the showers was an honest fixation. We both tended to key in on a particular subject that interested us and dig deep into it until there was nothing left to uncover. This meant Karen's attention towards a subject generally burned intensely before quickly fizzling out. My refusal to indulge her one last wish and take her to *The Showers* kept that fire going. She would strategically pick the moments where I was just drunk enough to loosen my lips but not *so* drunk that I was lost on the shores of oblivion to ask me questions about the story.

Occasionally, she brought up pieces of information I had told her while blacked out that would resonate with me enough to put me on edge for days on end. Even if I couldn't conjure the complete memories while sober, my body recognized them on some subconscious level. I knew that she was constantly treading closer to something in me that I didn't want to address, but I never stopped her outright. I don't know if I even believed my own story by that point; I just knew that I started feeling a bit sick every time it came up. She persisted—using every method in the book to convince me to take her to Broken Bow. Every new detail I revealed, fictitious or otherwise, would motivate her to push me harder.

It was the middle of winter when I finally caved.

At the time, we were living in Fort Collins, Colorado, which was a relatively short drive from Broken Bow. I had held my ground regarding returning to *The Showers* for so long that my responses were almost reflexive at that point. I claimed that we didn't have the time and that I had forgotten exactly how to get there—both of which were partially true. But, like I said, she knew when she could get to me.

One night, we found ourselves lounging on the couch following a long night of bar-hopping and friend drama. For once, we had found ourselves on the same side of the night's issue, which meant things might end on a rare, quiet note. We snuggled under a blanket and watched the Coen Brothers' *Inside Llewyn Davis*. While Karen watched intently, I split my time between nodding off and attempting to read a screenplay that a friend of mine had sent me. I'd seen the film a half-dozen times then, so I wasn't paying my full attention. In it, a struggling folk singer loses his way after his partner commits suicide. *Spoilers*, I guess.

Karen and I shared a mutual, morbid fascination with the subject of suicide, so it was only a matter of time before one of us said something about it.

"I would hate to jump off a bridge, I think," she said. "There's a chance you'd live after hitting the water, and you'd wind up, what, paralyzed or something? I guess I'd feel like an even bigger waste of space if I couldn't even manage to kill myself." I wasn't sure if she actually wanted to get into that conversation, but I bit anyway.

"I couldn't jump," I said, pulling her close, setting the script on the coffee table, and shutting my eyes. "There's way too much buildup and pressure. Then, once you get the balls to finally do it, there's a lot of time to regret it as you're falling."

It might seem unusual to some, but suicide wasn't a taboo subject between the two of us. It's difficult to explain to those unfamiliar with lifelong suicidal ideation, but discussing it in blunt and honest terms is comforting in a strange way. When faced with the struggle every day of your life, familiarizing yourself with something often considered macabre was its own sort of victory. It felt like discussing it shined a bright light on it—"know your enemy" and whatnot.

"Even if it were concrete or lava below me, I couldn't do it," I said. "I don't want anything flashy, honestly. Give me a bottle of benzos and a couple pints of *Chivas*, and I'll go gentle."

"Maybe I would jump," Karen thought out loud. "But I would do it from a plane. I just want that one last rush of adrenaline."

"You could stay alive and get a lot more of that," I replied.

"Not with those kinds of stakes," she said. She had a point.

"I just want mine to be quiet; I want the background noise to fade slowly into silence. Let me drink myself to death with a book and some relaxing music to play me out before that," I sighed. "I'd probably put on some *Bright Eyes* or *Elliott Smith* – I don't know." Karen was quiet for a while after that. A character in the film had just overdosed in a bathroom stall when she spoke up.

"I just don't want to go like that," she said. "At the very least, I'd want to be around friends or even family if no one else is available." I had begun nodding off. "Kind of like your teacher."

I stirred. She hadn't mentioned the story in a while, and whenever she did, she never led into it with Mr. Mays.

"I guess," I said. I slumped down onto a pillow and closed my eyes. I figured that if I fell asleep, she would have to leave the subject alone for the night.

"Let's go, bub," she said.

"Go where?" I asked.

"You know," Karen said. I did know.

"Liquor store's closed," I grumbled.

"No! *Nebraska*."

"It's a bit late—"

"Next week. I'll take it off work," Karen suggested. "I'll get someone to drive us."

"Why would anyone want to drive us to Nebraska?"

"Brian seems interested."

"In *Nebraska?*"

"I'm Interested in your story, dummy. You could write about it!" Karen said, looking for anything she could use to get me on board. "It's been a while since you've written. I could bring my camera. From the way you described it, I'm sure that I can get some good pictures." I was growing more uncomfortable with each passing second, but the anxiety was offset by my exhaustion.

"I don't want to go," I moaned. I didn't put up much of a fight.

"Please. For me?" she begged. "We never go anywhere, and the apartment gets stuffy, and it is my birthday next month."

"Okay, alright," I said, trying to appease her so I could drift off, "but what about the cat?"

The next thing I knew, our bags were packed, and we were leaving the comforts of my apartment for Nebraska. After I had agreed to the trip, I fell asleep. By the time I woke up the following afternoon, Karen had already secured one of her friends as our chauffeur and was requesting time off work that matched my schedule. She was happier than I had seen her in ages, and I was on quite a bit of Xanax, so I was looking for anything that might keep the good times rolling. Happiness was sometimes hard to come by with our schedules and changing moods. I kept that in the forefront of my mind as we loaded up the car.

I fell asleep before we made it out of town and woke up in what felt like another dimension. Outside my window, I saw only icy tundra that burned my eyes to look at; I hadn't seen that much sun in months. The reflection of the sun off of the snow only amplified it.

Our mutual friend Brian sat behind the wheel of my crummy 2005 Ford Escape as we flew down the interstate toward Broken Bow, Nebraska. Everyone called him the "responsible" one of our group of friends because he refused to get behind the wheel after drinking any booze at all. What only Karen and I knew was that he would often be high as a kite while driving us home and lecturing us on how he was the only one of us not destined for a DUI. But he had never been in an accident and never even received so much as a parking ticket, so we didn't say a word.

Karen sat shotgun with a large Styrofoam cup from Sonic resting in her lap. Knowing her, I assumed she had poured out three-quarters of the drink and filled the rest of the cup with vodka. After a minute, she noticed that I was awake.

"Hey, bub! Sleep well?" she asked, turning around in her seat to face me. A whiff of vodka with a hint of cherry limeade flooded my nostrils and burned my eyes. My guess was correct.

Karen refused to travel long distances without what she affectionately called a "roadie." She had adopted the term from her late father, Randy, who had killed himself when she was fourteen. He had opened his wrists over the sink in the bathroom while Karen was doing homework in her upstairs bedroom, and her mom was fucking a co-worker in her office at work. Her preoccupation with suicide at least came from somewhere logical.

She had always idolized her dad and hadn't spoken to her mother in a decade. She told me the story often—reinforcing the idea that any of her idiosyncrasies related to Randy (read: bad habits) were exempt from criticism. I made my only sensible move in that situation.

"Did you get me one?" I asked with a smile.

"Extra cup is for you, my dear. Half and half," She winked and handed me the Styrofoam cup of cure-all. It was much needed.

My jaw throbbed incessantly. I always had a problem with grinding my teeth in my sleep. It was so bad growing up that my canines actually grew outward and resembled vampire fangs by the time I entered high school. The grinding hadn't been an issue in quite a while, though. I figured that the previous night of partying, along with the anxiety about the trip, had taken a toll. The first sip of the drink made me wince; it was about one-quarter limeade to three-quarters cheap vodka.

"*Burnetts?*" I groaned and took another drink. "I guess it fits the scenery." Karen laughed.

Nothing except the frost-covered remains of the fall harvest and frozen dirt surrounded us for miles. I looked out over the repetitive backdrop for several hours. Barren earth occasionally gave way to tufts of shorn trees that reached futilely upwards towards the grey heavens. They resembled petrified roots that had aggressively snuffed out any hint of life that had once inhabited their numbers. Occasionally, I could spot the rusting remnants of a vehicle or a crumbling shed hidden among the branches – waiting patiently to be overtaken by the vindictive woodland.

The three of us passed the time by fiddling with a frayed tape-to-auxiliary cord converter so that we could play music on our phones. Unfortunately, even when we had gotten that to work, it was still a crapshoot, thanks to the spotty 4G connection in the plains.

Karen and I chain-smoked *Camel Crush* cigarettes, much to Brian's chagrin. He smoked too but would only touch the baby blue packs of *American Spirits*, which were "all-natural" and burned for an eternity. Smoking anything else, he believed, was just asking for cancer.

The drive was familiar and had me wandering through foggy memories of my last trip to Broken Bow. The haze left me frustrated and increasingly uncomfortable. Brian and Karen – despite having heard the story of *The Showers* tens of times by this point – prodded me for new details once we had crossed the state line into Nebraska. I dodged their inquisition by telling them how it was a violation of tradition to listen to a band while on the way to their concert. That shut them up and eased the pressure somewhat, but my teeth still ground against each other, and my jaw ached. Driving through Nebraska was awakening something in me—I felt anxious, defensive, and oddly sensitive, physically and emotionally.

Brian had grown up in New Jersey and, despite the relative emptiness of the two-lane highway we found ourselves on that morning, was driving like he was still there. I had no problems sweeping across lanes without a signal, speeding, or jerking left and right to exit the interstate on any regular day. As uncomfortable as it might be to avoid the eye contact of an angry truck driver that Brian had cut off, we always reached our destination much faster than the GPS estimate. But that day, his highway practices made me queasy. The honks from several angry passersby got to be too much, so I threw in my headphones and pulled my beanie over my eyes in an attempt at sensory deprivation. It allowed me to drift off after a bit.

I hadn't remembered my dreams in years, but I sure as hell remember the nightmare I had in the back seat of my car that day.

I was back at the bar near Cayuga Heights in New York—the same place where I had last met Mr. Mays almost a decade before. The faceless patrons' muted voices hummed in the air, and the neon beer signs buzzed around us. I sat next to my deceased former teacher, who was sporting the sweater that read, "I'm the birthday boy."

Mr. Mays looked up at me from the depths of a drink. His eyes were bloodshot from holding his booze and holding back tears. He didn't say anything, but the conversation between us from years ago rang through my head—growing loud enough to fill the quiet space as the memory sharpened. I remembered his friend—the one he had lost at *The Showers*. Mr. Mays looked away from me and into his drink. He didn't look back up.

The sound of dripping water echoed around the bar. Looking before me, I found a highball glass filled to the brim with whiskey. Without a second thought, I threw it back. I felt the familiar, calming burn in my gut. I pursed my lips and sat it back on the table as the lights around the bar dimmed from the outside in. I rubbed my eyes and breathed deeply to quell the burn, but it worsened.

The room continued to dim as the dripping noise rang around me, growing louder with each subsequent drop. Looking up at the glass before me, I saw it had filled again—the liquid still rippling from a recent pour. Another drop fell from above, breaking the surface tension and spilling the drink all over the bar top. I looked up to see a showerhead hanging just beyond the light – the source of the liquid. Trembling pipes echoed around me, and the showerhead began to shake violently. It erupted as I jolted back to reality—panicking and thrashing about for a moment. My knee and arm cracked loudly as I moved about and adjusted to the real world.

"Woah, bubs. Easy now," Karen said with a chuckle. We were parked at a rest stop. Brian had pulled in with excess haste and hit the curb hard, which had woken me up. I tasted Cherry Limeade crawling up my esophagus and felt my stomach rumble.

"We're outside of Hastings. Don't know how far. Use the restroom now or forever hold your pees," said Karen.

When I opened the car door, the icy wind pushed it back against me, slamming hard against my foot. Annoyed, I pushed harder and slipped out. I quickly jogged across the lot and into the unexpected bustle of the rest area.

I tried to ignore the sounds of showers in the stalls at the back of the room as I did my business and washed my hands. It was difficult to dismiss the feeling of every drop in my chest. I couldn't tell if I was hallucinating, experiencing remnants from my nightmare, or if the sounds really were *that* loud. Anxiety like that hadn't gotten to me so bad in ages.

The residual nausea that followed me from the dream caused me to gag as I approached the sink to wash my hands. I closed my eyes and took deep breaths as I pulled a flask from my jacket pocket. I looked around me to gauge the level of judgment I was about to receive. The truckers didn't seem to take a second glance. But, a father in the middle changing his infant at the station near the door shot me a dirty look. Maybe he didn't. I'm not sure why I cared; it wouldn't stop me.

One of the showers in the back turned on full blast. My chest tightened. I took a pull from the flask, and my stomach relaxed, causing the gagging to cease. I cleared my throat of whatever had built up before the nip of whiskey and spit it into the sink. What came out was a bright shade of red. I didn't panic; a little bit of blood just meant that I had forgotten to eat for a day or two. It wasn't anything significant.

I returned to the car after pushing back through the line of people gathered at the restroom door. Karen was sitting inside with the window cracked—holding a dying cigarette halfway out the window. When she saw me, she flicked it out and rolled the window up—gesturing for me to hurry. I hopped inside, and we were back on the interstate within seconds.

"Don't fall asleep on us again, bub. We're going to need you to steer us from here," Karen said.

"Just get us to Broken Bow," I said, staring out over some of the harvested fields that looked like they had been burnt. "I'll guide us from there." I had become something of a tour guide, I supposed.

We continued down the interstate for quite some time while Brian and Karen sang songs. I sat in the backseat, working on grounding myself. My anxiety was manifesting as an intense aching in my gut coupled with heartburn that moved all the way up my esophagus. I attempted to drown the acidic taste out of my mouth with vodka, Tums, and a couple of Xanax I had stashed in my bag. The combination helped me to forget about the pain, at least.

"We're going to need some gas if we plan on hunting for this place in the boonies all night," said Brian.

"Well, there are only about ten gas stations in the state, so exit where you can," I said. I caught the tail end of a sign that read "Broken Bow" but didn't catch the other information. Within minutes, Brian exited the highway and pulled into what appeared to be a gas station. It had the pumps out front and a small convenience store. Behind it was a rickety single-story house—its Victorian design faded and chipped to all hell. Some windows looked busted in, and the holes were stuffed with assorted cloths and rags. I felt a sense of recognition as I stepped out of the car into the increasingly frigid wind and began to pump gas. Karen ran inside to grab snacks as Brian shouted after her.

"Get me sunflower seeds," he yelled. Karen was already inside. Brian looked at me, "Jack, sunflower seeds? Please, and thanks, man." He closed the car door before I could say I wasn't planning on going inside. I grumbled as I walked into the old station. I figured he *was* our designated driver, so I couldn't get too upset with him barking orders. I was just irritable and all over the place.

The building had a familiar musty smell, which, to my surprise, helped to clear away some of the haze that I was stuck in. I was pretty sure it was a gas station I'd visited before. It wasn't unlikely, considering where we were at and the aforementioned sparsity of stops in the area. *It was a neat coincidence.* That's what I told myself, at least.

Karen stood up at the counter, making pleasant conversation about something or another with a girl who couldn't have been much older than twenty. She was pretty in that "country bumpkin" sort of way. Her dirty-blonde hair was haphazardly thrown up in a ponytail, and her clothes were faded. She wore a faded yellow t-shirt and torn denim jeans; both items lacked any identifiable brand name. She stood in stark contrast with Karen, whose every item of clothing and accessory popped with so many different colors that she looked like a paint set. Everything about the girl at the counter seemed almost intentionally indistinct, washed out, and vague. If I had seen her face today, I don't think I would have known her from Eve. She blended right in with the browns and greys of her surroundings. If I had to guess, I would have said that she was likely born and raised in the house behind the gas station and had no intentions of ever leaving Broken Bow, Nebraska.

I must have stared at her for a moment too long because as the two carried on their conversation, the girl's eyes darted directly toward me. I was taken aback by how completely unsubtle she was about it. She somehow didn't miss a beat in their conversation; Karen carried on without pause and only glanced my way for a split second. I'm sure that I looked anxious and sweaty from the booze, pills, and stress, so I didn't blame her for keeping an eye on me. But, the unflinching nature of her gaze threw me off. The sunlight poured through the windows and bounced off of her eyes in such a way that when I would briefly look up at her, all that stood out were two tiny glints of light pointed like daggers in my direction.

I attempted to work the pain out of my jaw muscles with my knuckles as I wandered the aisles. I had just about given in to the discomfort. I headed towards the exit when I heard Karen ask the young lady at the counter, point blank, "What do you know about *The Showers?*"

Again, the girl didn't miss a single beat.

"People don't deal with anything related to that sort of business around here anymore," she said softly. My legs froze up, and I turned my head towards her. She seemed to be speaking directly to me. "That was all a long time ago," she said.

Her eyes remained locked on mine. The pain in my jaw pulsed, and my stomach lurched. Consciously and unconsciously, I rejected the overwhelming feeling of déjà vu. I raced for the small hallway in the back of the store. I held my stomach and refused to look up at the girl. I could still feel her gaze on me. Karen continued to press her unsuccessfully for information.

I managed to get through the door and locked it behind me before falling to my knees in front of the toilet. My stomach clenched over and over again. Nothing came out as I dry heaved and struggled to catch a breath. With the pressure behind my eyes and skull building, I shoved my finger down my throat. I was convinced I would feel better if I could purge *anything at all*. I choked on my finger until I saw stars and finally gave up. I didn't need to pass out in a gas station bathroom. That sounded too close to rock bottom for comfort.

My body was glazed with sweat as I sat back on the restroom floor and concentrated on deep breathing exercises to get my vision to stabilize and my heartbeat to slow. I had picked the exercises up while googling anxiety symptoms late one stressful night; they were a grounding technique for panic attacks and had never worked for me in the past. But I was desperate, and, to my surprise, they worked.

The pressure in my head slowly released as I wiped away the torrent of tears that had wet my face. My eyes aimlessly wandered the room, eventually landing on a green picture frame next to the mirror above the sink. It read, "You can't choose 'em. You just gotta love 'em," and housed a photo of what appeared to be three generations of women laughing while posing outside of a large green farmhouse. I recognized the youngest of the three as the girl at the counter outside. Standing beside the girl was a woman I believed to be her mother. Behind those two stood a sweet-looking older woman in a sundress—the same dress she had been wearing when I ventured into that gas station with my friend Steve many years ago.

The three of us had a pleasant conversation about the town and our post-college trip until our motives for staying in Broken Bow were made clear. When she discovered that we were searching for *The Showers*, her demeanor changed drastically. She gave us a stern and measured answer that stuck with me throughout the years. It sounded distinctly rehearsed to me then; it had sounded *scripted*.

"People don't deal with anything relating to that sort of business around here anymore," she told us. "That was all a long time ago."

I rose to my feet – head spinning – and splashed several handfuls of water on my face. A capillary had burst in my right eye. It was blood red, dilated, and raining tears. I was a mess, but I couldn't bring myself to care. After spitting up a bit of blood into the sink, I shuffled out of the restroom and into the hallway. Before walking away, I shot one last glance back at the photo to confirm I wasn't just imagining things. It was still the same old woman standing outside the same green farmhouse.

I rushed towards the front door with shaking legs—knocking bags of sunflower seeds and sticks of beef jerky onto the floor along the way. Karen was still talking with the girl at the counter. I didn't think the girl was staring at me anymore, but I didn't look up to confirm. *Was she ever really staring at me, or was I just losing it?*

I was a few steps from the door before Karen noticed me. She looked me up and down with a concerned look and put a reassuring hand on my back. The comfort of her touch sent goosebumps across my body, and I shivered.

"You feeling okay, bub?" asked Karen. The girl at the counter stared at her with a suddenly vacant look. "Did you get sick?" I looked at Karen, then at the girl, at Karen again, out towards the car, and back at Karen once more.

"Must have eaten something bad," I said, looking up at the girl without making eye contact. "Sensitive stomach." I watched her chin bob up and down as she nodded. I couldn't tell if the look in her eyes was one of understanding or one of suspicion.

"Thanks-have-a-good-day," I said, bolting out the door. The bell above me rang; I could feel it resonate in my jaw. Karen quickly followed me after giving the girl some sort of excuse for my behavior.

"Hey!" Karen caught up with me before I got to the car, "What's up with you?"

"I'm just tired," I told her. She saw through the lie instantly and raised an eyebrow, waiting for a more honest response. "I took a nip that went down the wrong pipe and got a little sick. It happens. Just wanted to avoid her... *judgy* eyes." I gestured back towards the door. The girl no longer stood behind the counter. "This is Jesus' country, and I feel like she would try to walk me through a twelve-step pamphlet or something." Karen seemed content with my answer. "I'm not looking to get saved right now." She laughed.

We continued towards the car, and I took a few more deep breaths. My lungs burned. The temperature felt like it had dropped while we were in the gas station, and the layer of sweat on my skin felt like it was starting to freeze. Karen stole my attention from the cold.

"Who needs Jesus when you have me as your guardian angel?" Karen asked with a cartoonish smile and exaggerated wink.

I faked a gagging sound.

"You're gonna make me sick again," I said.

Karen kissed me on the cheek and hopped into the passenger seat.

Brian put on a Dandy Warhols album and jammed by himself.

"I'd like to thank you, my dear. In less than a year," he sang, poorly. He reached his hand back towards me, expecting something in return. "Sunflower, see–" He stopped himself the instant he saw my face. "Never...mind, then! Alright, are we good to go, team?"

Karen took control of the phone and switched the song. *Bohemian Like You* blasted through the car stereo.

"Let's bounce," she said. She threw on her sunglasses and lit a cigarette.

I tried my best not to look back as we drove away from the gas station and deeper into the Nebraskan hinterlands.

PART IV

THE NIGHTMARE OF MY CHOICE

MARCH 13TH, 2018

The three of us spent another hour and a half aimlessly driving around the outskirts of Broken Bow. I was giving directions to nowhere in particular while still thinking about the girl from the gas station. It felt entirely possible that the whole coincidence was my imagination getting away from me. My mind could have been filling gaps in my memory with strange, fictitious ideas. Even if it was the same gas station owned by the same family, why did that matter? There were only a handful of gas stations around that area; I had said so myself earlier in the day. I remembered something Steve had mentioned long ago about locals messing with people who invade their towns in search of urban legends. Maybe that canned, scripted phrase was how that family dealt with it.

I was trying to push the other oddities from that encounter out of my mind with another drink when I spotted a familiar oasis on the horizon. Karen and Brian had yet to notice. My stomach sank, my blood ran cold, and my vision became a tunnel. I had somehow steered us there without realizing it; that was the only explanation

I could muster. I had absolutely no fucking clue where we were, but we still wound up *there*.

Maybe you had to get lost to find them. Perhaps they sought me out.

I kept my eyes down and stayed quiet. My thoughts raced, and I began to feel lightheaded. Another anxiety attack slowly crept up on me – one symptom at a time. I hoped that if I said nothing, we would just drive right by that patch of forest, eventually call it a day, and let *The Showers* fade from our lives forever.

Brian turned the wheel toward the trees without a word of guidance from me.

At that moment, I began to realize how desperately I had wanted to avoid that place. I didn't want to go back at all, and I vowed never to go back there. I could feel myself saturating my two T-shirts and hoodie with sweat while I attempted to keep my composure.

"Maybe we can call it a night and try again some other time," I stuttered. The words fell out of my mouth. They were slurred and almost robotic sounding.

"I'm going to try that ominous-looking patch of trees over there first," said Brian. But after that, I'm down for whatever you guys want to do. I'm getting a little tired anyway."

I fixated on the tree line as we gradually worked our way across the bumpy terrain of the previously undisturbed field. I could feel the pull of the farmhouse and the tunnels at the heart of that little forest. The naked trees shimmered in the setting sun's light, but the sight was more foreboding than comforting. The branches extended outward as if reaching for the car – beckoning us.

"Shit, bub, this is looking pretty *Evil Dead*," Karen said. "Ringing any bells?"

"This is the place," I said.

The words went through my mind and out of my mouth in less than a second. I hardly even tried to stop them. Karen and Brian both celebrated with quiet *oohs*; I tore at my fingernails with my teeth.

I promised myself I would never again step near Broken Bow. Still, I would be lying if I said I had never imagined that homecoming. I thought a lot about some imaginary brave version of myself returning to the scene of my personal horror show in search of answers. I'd come out of it with an actual ending for the saga of *The Showers* – actual explanations for what I saw there. Maybe I could break a story about the nefarious nature of whatever happened in that place. Over the years, I spent a long time thinking about these hypotheticals and forming theories about what *The Showers* were. But, eventually, the effort seemed pointless.

A part of them existed only within the confines of my story – what I posted on the internet and had chosen to tell the world. With only my account to go on, *The Showers* were a hundred different things to a hundred different people. It was a meeting place for a violent ritualistic cult to some. It was a site for experiments performed by the KKK or deeply rooted Nazis (post-World War II) for others. To many, mine was just another ghost story about a haunted farmhouse in Bumfuck, Nebraska, and that was enough. I'm not dense. I know that the real draw of my story lies in the fear of the unknown; ambiguous horror was my bread and butter for a long time. That was why the story resonated heavily with some people and left others disappointed; some people need those answers, and others would rather the mystery remain.

At the time, I didn't even know what I wanted from the place. For me, *The Showers* were far more complex. They existed outside of rational thought and comprehension because my experience with them partially robbed me of those attributes.

As the car rolled slowly through the thickening brush that winter evening, I sat silently in my seat. Despite my previous experience with *The Showers*—the story that I had recounted versions of hundreds of times—I had no idea what exactly we were moving towards.

Tree branches reached out and scraped against the car's exterior, forging new grooves and playing the metal like a warped record. The sharp, grinding sounds felt like they were splitting my skull in two. I put in my noise-canceling earbuds and tried to focus on anything else. Brian winced as the branches dug into the car, looking back at me apologetically. Karen stared at our surroundings like a kid who had just stepped foot into an amusement park for the first time.

Abandon all hope, ye who enter here.

Several troubling thoughts flooded my mind as we drew nearer to the clearing. I never really had a choice in making that trip. I would always end up back there, one way or another. I began to feel that the entire series of events was predetermined. Every time I told my story – Mr. Mays' story – I inched further along the path that would eventually pull me back to *The Showers*. Every drink I took to forget those tunnels, every girl I slept with to distract from the ceaseless nightmares, and every addition to the story I conjured up to distance myself from the reality of what happened to me there just further sealed my fate. I was free to leave Broken Bow, return home, and have all of the booze and noncommittal sex my body could handle. But every action I took was another futile attempt at prolonging the inevitable.

As a kid, I had accomplished exactly what I tried to do with urban legends: *I put myself into the story.* In doing so, I had forever bound myself to that place – and it to me. *The Showers* and I were inextricably linked, and I forged that link willingly. The simple truth was this: I was always going to return to that clearing, that farmhouse, and those tunnels because they were sitting there, waiting for me – and they were *patient.*

Brian stopped the car abruptly, just short of the large clearing hiding at the small forest's center. In front of us sat the monstrous, rotting carcass of a tree that was far too large to have grown out in the middle of Nebraska. It had decomposed considerably since my last visit, but I recognized it all the same. I took a deep breath. *One last chance to back out – the point of no return.*

"I could probably get us over this, but I've already scratched the shit out of your car, and this might do a number on her undercarriage," Brian said.

"We can walk," Karen said, pulling her coat from the backseat.

"You guys can walk," said Brian. "I have some smoking to do." He smiled and brandished a small baggie of weed that he pulled seemingly out of thin air. I looked at Karen, confused; she stared at Brian with a similar expression.

"We came all this way, and you're going to stay in the car?" Karen asked.

"It's the journey, not the destination, Karen," he said, grinning. "Besides, somebody has to keep the car warm. Just yell for me if you find anything spooky." Karen looked pissed. Brian didn't seem to care. Neither of them moved for a few silent seconds. Brian slowly grabbed his grinder from the center console without breaking eye contact. His smile widened as Karen's face reddened. He was egging her on. But Karen had been more upset with him about less before. He knew it would pass.

"Make good decisions," he whispered. With a giggle, he turned up the music and turned on the high beams on the headlights.

Karen exited the car without another word. I followed, shooting Brian an annoyed but understanding look as I closed the car door.

Karen was already circling around the fallen tree. I pushed back my bubbling anxiety and ran forward to keep up with her.

"So what do you think?" I asked. I wanted to get her talking instead of dwelling on Brian. Karen put one hand on the mountain of crumbling timber and pulled a small plastic bottle of vodka from her jacket.

"We're not even on the ride yet," she said, grinning sarcastically. She took a long pull from the bottle. The setting sun caught the plastic just right, and a ray of light momentarily blinded me. My head throbbed, and I winced. When I looked back up, she had moved out of the way, and I could see into the clearing. There it was – or rather, wasn't. The massive farmhouse that had once occupied the space was nowhere to be found. There was nothing in the clearing but the same undisturbed dirt that made up every other empty field in the state. Karen took notice as we stepped out into the barren expanse.

"It seems a bit empty," she said, obviously disappointed. "Are you sure this is it?"

I was sure, though it took me a moment to respond. My brain was still trying to tackle the impossible emptiness that stood before me.

"It's, uh, definitely," I stuttered.

I pulled my flask from my jacket and sipped from it while I walked the perimeter of the clearing. My eyes were constantly drawn back to where I was certain a massive farmhouse had once stood. I ran through numerous explanations in my head. The situation wasn't impossible; old buildings are torn down all the time. But I had questions. *Who had done it? When? Did this mean it wasn't abandoned when I had been there before?* I couldn't wrap my mind around the situation. At the very least, there should have been remnants of the farmhouse or evidence that the tunnels had been filled at some point. There should have been a path in the trees carved for the equipment they would have undoubtedly needed to clear the structure. But, the clearing and surrounding forest was undisturbed and as thick as it had been when I had last visited in the middle of summer.

Still, I was sure we were in the right place; I could feel it. The peaceful quiet of the trees and the calming glow of the frosted ground were just part of a front. It had put on a nice face to hide itself from me. I took a lengthy pull from my flask.

It was then that the real bareness of that place dawned on me. Brian was in the car; Karen wandered the clearing in a circle, spiraling towards the center; I continued to stay along the tree line. We were the only occupants in that space like germs sucked into a vast vacuum. There were no deer, birds, rodents, or bugs to be found. There were no tracks or scat. I hadn't seen so much as a spider web in the trees as we had moved through them. It was winter, but surely something should have been living in that place. The clearing was completely desolate – a landscape frozen in time and devoid of life. It might have been picturesque if I had escaped the feeling of impending calamity.

"So where's the giant 'X'?" asked Karen. She stumbled around the open space, looking bored and frustrated. Her nose had turned bright from the cold. Her cheeks began to match, turning a darker shade of scarlet with every pull she took from her bottle of vodka. We had only been there for twenty minutes. The sun had almost disappeared behind the trees. Her bottle was practically empty.

"Not here, I guess," I responded with a fake sigh of disappointment. I moved towards the car indirectly, trying my best to be subtle. I wanted to leave there before that place could reveal its true self. The pressure in the clearing built, and a mosquito-like buzzing rang in my ear. I felt as if I were standing helplessly in front of a massive jack-in-the-box and watching the handle slowly turn.

"I don't know. It has been over a decade, after all," I said.

"There *has* to be something here," Karen moaned. "If the place was as big as you said, something would have to be left."

"I'm not sure how big it actually was, thinking back on it," I said. "It's like visiting your old elementary school after a few years and being able to touch the ceiling." By this point, I was closing in on the car, directly across the clearing from Karen. She circled me broadly, running around and kicking at the ground, her eyes peeled wide.

"The tunnels, though!" she yelled. "The cellar door!"

"It's a big space." I shrugged my shoulders. "Trees could have overtaken it. The tunnels could have been filled or collapsed. They weren't the most stable things in the first place," I said, rambling on in an attempt to explain my way out of the situation. "Maybe someone found out that Steve and I had come out here and didn't want anyone else trespassing afterward. Those tunnels could have been a death trap for stupid kids looking to go urban exploring." Karen stopped moving when she noticed where I was headed.

"What are you doing, bub?" she asked. "Where are you going?" She held the now-empty bottle of vodka at her side. I could see the top of another one peeking out of her breast pocket.

"Gonna go get warm," I explained casually and calmly. "If it's gone, it's gone. It's probably for the best anyway. I hurt myself pretty bad las-"

"Come the *fuck* on," she said, frustration showing in her voice. "We didn't drive hours and hours just to leave after ten minutes." She stared at me. Her gaze was piercing, and I avoided contact with her bloodshot eyes as best as I could.

"It was a nice little road trip. But I don't feel well, it's cold as shit, and it's getting dark, babe." I put my hands in my coat and continued towards the car. I could see Brian's silhouette with a bong in his hand amidst a cloud of smoke that had filled the entire vehicle.

"Well, that's some *bullshit*," Karen grumbled from behind me. I turned around to face her, giving in and making eye contact. She had opened the second bottle of vodka. With a flourish, she took the empty bottle and whipped it over my head into the trees. I didn't break eye contact as I heard it smack against a tree in the distance with a hollow *clunk*. Her every breath poured from her nostrils like smoke. It couldn't have been more than ten degrees outside. The sun was out of view. A deep, orange glow filled the sky at that moment, but it would soon disappear.

I felt my heart rate began to speed up. My hands began to shake with anxiety in addition to the chill. The pain that had been growing in my gut throughout the entire trip flared up once again. I knew it was just because of the stress. But it's difficult to breathe your way through an ulcer. I fell down to one knee. I felt like I was going to vomit fire. The ice on the ground had thinned beneath me. Only frost and hardened earth remained. My chest tightened.

"I think we should just go," I told Karen. The feeling of impending doom had built to a point where my nerves felt like they were about to explode. The ringing in my ears grew louder. I was on my way to full-blown panic. I needed to get out of that clearing.

"I think I need to go to urgent care, Karen," I said, bringing one arm across my stomach and holding it tight in a futile attempt to quell the burning.

"Fucking convenient," said Karen.

I froze. Even at our worst, she had never gone after me when she knew that I was having a panic attack. We both knew how bad things could get and how quickly our mental states could turn. She had never egged it on before.

"You're not getting your way, and so suddenly you pull the trump card," she yelled across the field. I could hear the vitriol in her voice.

"Okay, Jack. I'll take you to an urgent care in the middle of Kansas." She was mocking me. *It had to be the influence of that place.*

"Nebraska," I corrected. She looked at me like a bullet, and her body language shifted dramatically.

"Oh, I'm sorry," she said sarcastically, stepping towards me. "*Nebraska.* It's just that your story changes so fucking often that I don't know which parts of it are true and what parts are bullshit." She picked up a rock and whipped it into the trees. It wasn't thrown at me, but it was close enough that I considered it a warning shot. I heard it bounce off several trees, shattering ice along its path. My jaw popped. She had never been violent with me before. But, even with that in mind, I knew that if she got to it, her next throw wouldn't miss.

"Let's go to urgent care, Jack," Karen said. Her switch had flipped. "They can give you some Ativan and tell you that it's *just* a fucking panic attack again. *Then*, we are coming right back here." Karen and I had been together through enough of our rapid mood fluctuations that we knew how to handle one another when that sort of thing happened. I certainly knew how to respond to her in a way that would make the whole situation more manageable for both of us. I also knew *exactly* which buttons to push to set her off. At that moment, I wasn't feeling particularly diplomatic.

"Stop being a fucking dick, Karen," I yelled back at her. The pain in my head and stomach was getting to me. *That place* was getting to both of us.

She stepped towards me with purpose.

"What in the fuck did you just-" she began before a dull and hollow *thud* rang out from beneath her boot. It was her turn to freeze.

I didn't bother to look up. I knew exactly what the noise was; it was familiar. Karen looked down to find a large set of wooden cellar doors buried in the dirt, debris, and ice. She dropped down and quickly brushed them off with her boots and bare hands. I stayed on the ground and kept my head down as she worked.

"Let's just go, Karen," I begged. "Please, let's just go."

"What's down..." she said, trailing off as she scraped at the ice.

After a couple of minutes, she stopped. I heard the loud crackle of ice and wood accompanied by Karen's strained groans. I looked up just as a cellar door the size of a pallet fell to the ground with a resonant *thud*. The ice below it splintered outwards, creating a web of deep, dark cracks in the ground. Karen stood triumphant above the massive hole. She stared into the darkness with intense curiosity and determination in her eyes.

The orange glow in the sky had turned to black. We sat in silence for several moments under the pale light of a half-moon; the dim emanation was swallowed by the assailing darkness of the pit.

"We have to leave," I pleaded. "Please, Karen."

"What's down there?" she asked. Her eyes were still fixed on the hole.

"No," I said. I struggled to breathe. A rush of memories flooded back, but the pieces were mixed up and disjointed. I couldn't make sense of them. My thoughts ran through my head so rapidly that I could hardly form more than one word at a time. "Please. No."

"What is down there," she repeated again. Her gaze began to jump between me and the pit. "What's down there?!" Her voice rose against my silence. "Come on, Jack. Tell me a story! We came all this way for this. So, if you expect me to walk away from it right now, then you better weave a slick fucking story, bub."

I looked up at her, hoping that she could see the desperation in my eyes. I wanted her to understand what that place had done to my head and why I wanted to turn around and go home. I hoped she could see how badly I did not want to face that place. She either couldn't see it, or she didn't care. I didn't know which was worse.

"Make something up, Hemingway!" she yelled. "What do you call a writer that doesn't write, Jack?"

I was depressed and panicking and drunk and stuck in a tornado of disjointed thoughts. Karen was actively *trying* to hurt me. I planted my hand on the ground and pushed myself to my feet. I realized that my fingers had gone numb. She was baiting me at that point, and I bit – hard.

"Oh, fuck you," I said. Karen raised an eyebrow. I think she might have even smirked as I began to yell. "You made me do this! I *never* wanted to come back here. *You* made me come back, and now you're gonna chastise me because it doesn't live up to *your* expectations?" I felt tears begin to fall down my cheek. They quickly froze in place.

"It's just a fucking story, Karen—a *horror* story. Horror as in afraid; I'm *afraid*," I cried. I looked for any hint of empathy in her eyes and found none. At that moment, she was not the Karen that I knew. "You weren't fucking there, so you don't fucking know! You don't know what happened." She crossed her arms. I think she thought I was spinning another story. "I made *some* shit up! I did! For you and every other girl I told it to." She didn't react to that like I wanted. I felt angry. I wanted to hurt her back, and she was denying me the satisfaction.

"I would never," I said, taking a deep breath. I paused and locked eyes with her. I wanted to make sure that my next statement landed. "I would never – in a million *fucking* years – drag you back to your dad's house."

Karen's shoulders dropped, and her gaze shifted to the dirt at her feet. Guilt washed over me instantaneously. I had drawn a line and crossed it with a single slurred sentence. The momentum that she had built in the preceding several minutes stopped completely. The energy visibly drained from her body. We stood in that clearing in silence for several more minutes. I was afraid to move.

After a deep breath, Karen stepped towards me. She filled the large gap between us quickly. In one swift motion, she planted her foot in front of me and punched me in the face. I felt very little.

"Tell me what you're so fucking afraid of, Jack," Karen said. She seethed and breathed through gritted teeth, staring a hole through my chest. I said nothing; it was my only course of action. "Big bad hero in your stories – facing down anything that comes in your way, right? Well, I'm standing right here, so tell me. What are you so afraid of that you would pull *that* out of the bag? What is so fucking scary that you would *end us* to avoid it?"

"I don't know," I uttered under my breath. I could feel myself begin to wobble and sway; it wasn't the booze. It felt like my body was confused—like my brain was playing catch up and had left everything else on standby.

"I don't know," I repeated. It was the honest truth. I had no idea what *exactly* waited in that tunnel. I couldn't even muster a vague description. I couldn't remember. I had spent so much time embellishing and lying about my experience at *The Showers* to entertain or reach certain ends that I had never really processed what had happened to me there. I never thought about how it changed my perception of myself or my perception of reality. I never *wanted* to think about it, so I never *had* to think about it.

I just turned it into a story while it ate away at me for years, unchecked. I took that story, and I spread it to entertain and people. Maybe I wanted to let it out so that I could feel better. Perhaps I wanted other people to feel what I felt – *the fear*. Either way, I did the same thing as Mr. Mays, just on a larger scale, thanks to the internet.

I lied. I distanced myself enough from the reality of the situation with the lies because it made the reality of what happened to me at *The Showers* easier to cope with. I thought I had everything under control.

But there I stood, forced to face reality. I never had control. I was *running*.

"It's a dark dirt fucking *pit* in the middle of fucking *Nebraska*, Jack!" Karen yelled, taunting me. When I didn't respond, she walked back towards the cellar door. She looked back at me again before taking a single step into the darkness. "I'm going in without you. Fuck it."

"Please don't!" I screamed. I was in the midst of a full-on panic attack. Fear, guilt, and shame were among the emotions overwhelming my brain. I couldn't articulate it.

What do you see, Jack? I remembered the voice that had taunted me as I sat helpless in the dark many years ago. I remembered the *horror*. But the details weren't all there yet.

Karen took two more steps into the darkness, and she was swallowed up to her hips. She grabbed the heavy wooden door and grunted as she lifted it once more.

"Don't wait up," she said with a grin. In the blink of an eye, she disappeared into the pit. The door fell behind her with a resounding *thump* and puff of dust.

The clearing fell silent. I heard bits of the frost-covered ground crackling quietly around me as my body heat escaped. Standing allowed me a view of my car's headlights glowing brightly in the distance. I was sure that Brian had passed out in the back by that point, wrapped in his sleeping bag. I didn't bother disturbing him.

It would have done no good to bring him down there with me. It wasn't his struggle to face.

I looked back towards the sealed cellar door. I couldn't hear anything from below.

I tried to convince myself that there wasn't a pressing need to go down there. If I stood quietly in the clearing, I had little doubt that Karen would emerge after a few minutes of roaming around in the dark – no worse for wear. She would have given me shit about being a coward. We would sleep it off in the car and return to our regular, chaotic life.

Maybe that was close enough.

I had returned to *The Showers* despite my fears, and maybe, I thought, I could finally let it go. Karen got to see the birthplace of the story that she obsessed over, and I believed that I had confronted whatever I needed to confront. Nothing more needed to be done. After all, the farmhouse was gone, the dead land was frozen solid, and the property looked abandoned entirely. *It would never take anyone again; it would never hurt anyone again; it could never hurt me again.* All I had to do was stand in front of those cellar doors and wait.

But I couldn't resist. I felt compelled to walk over and pry open the doors. I felt a mighty need – an itch that needed to be scratched even though the skin was already broken and bleeding. I couldn't help myself.

Within seconds, I was staring into the beckoning darkness. The dim moonlight struggled to pierce the black veil as I took my first careful step down, then another. The wooden door was heavier than I remembered. I braced it against my shoulder as I inched down the icy ramp. I watched as my feet disappeared before my eyes—swallowed by the inky black of the tunnel. It took my legs next, but I was helping it along. Even through thick pants and boots, the darkness felt a great deal colder than the clearing. My legs tensed like they had been submerged in ice water. The cold had crept up to my knees when I felt a familiar shooting pain in my right leg that I hadn't felt in years. I knew it was psychosomatic because it *had* to be. It ran up my leg so quickly that I grabbed it on reflex alone. I shifted my weight onto my left leg, which tried to root itself in a patch of black ice. I tumbled downward into the abyss. The wooden door fell behind me with a crash, snuffing out the last traces of light as the darkness consumed me.

The fall felt like it lasted for an eternity. When I finally landed, my shoulder took the brunt of the impact. My head hit second. My neck whipped, and my skull bounced hard against the ground. I think that I lost consciousness, but it was difficult to tell. The tunnels were silent, pitch black, and freezing cold, so the line between conscious and unconscious blurred. I don't know how long I lay there on the dirt floor, but I know I didn't want to move. I knew that I had to keep going. I rolled onto my back and felt the frozen ground through my coat. An involuntary groan escaped my mouth, but it sounded muted as if I were underwater.

My fingers were completely numb, and I struggled as I reached my bare hand into my pocket to grab my phone. I don't know what I was doing trying to walk down there without a light ready in the first place. I brought the phone to my face and pressed the home button. The display wasn't bright, but it hurt my eyes. The screen was shattered, a web of broken glass covering a picture of Karen and me—my phone's wallpaper. It was a selfie that she took of the two of us at any one of the numerous local breweries we frequented. Her eyes were closed and she was smirking while kissing me on the cheek. I was half smiling—my hair a greasy mess. My eyes were glazed and red; I wasn't a subtle drunk. I didn't remember the night.

The screen flashed a message about a corrupt SD card, followed by another about a low battery. The fall had done a number on it—more than I would have thought. I swiped my finger across the display, and the phone's flashlight came to life. Tiny pieces of fractured glass pushed their way into my thumb.

"Just get me through this, and I'll buy you a nice new screen," I whispered to the dying device. I felt like I needed to fill the silence with something. My voice sounded distant and muted to my own ears. I opened my jaw wide, causing it to pop four times in quick succession. It did little to alleviate the throbbing in my temples.

I turned my light forward into the tunnel. My phone was either dying or those tunnels were eating the light – keeping it from showing me more than it wanted me to see. Little bits of my memory rushed back into my head. Gaps in my memory began filling at such a rapid pace that it made me dizzy. *Were they really gaps, though?* No, they were just memories pushed aside – overlooked, ignored, *covered up*. My leg began to throb again, just like it had when I fell through the floor of a farmhouse so many years ago. I wondered if that hole was still there—holding onto the piece of denim that it stole from my jeans. I began to move deeper into the tunnel.

I heard shuffling behind me, in front of me, and all around me. Every movement I made was slow, careful, and deliberate. With each step, there would be a brief silence followed by the echo of another step. The tunnels were too small; *they had no echo.* I tried my best not to let myself get more worked up than I already was. I might as well have been yelling at a fire to put it out.

As I began to find a groove in my cautious movement through the cavern, the light from my phone flickered twice. I held my breath and onto hope. With a final flash of the "low battery" symbol, it died. Feeling set back but not defeated, I chucked my phone into the pitch black. I didn't hear it hit a thing. I pressed onwards. My hand glided along the ceiling to keep me from running into walls or wooden crossbeams in the darkness.

A putrid stench like death and rot slowly crawled its way into my nostrils. It burned my eyes and made my stomach clench in an involuntary attempt to purge itself. Much to my dismay, I only gagged. The smell instantly ignited large parts of my memory. It was like the smell of your mother's home-cooked dinner, causing a rush of associated childhood memories to flood your head. But, instead of feeling comfort at the familiarity, I felt confused. I hadn't thought about that awful smell in years. But it had always been right there. *How had I let it get away from me? How had I let any of the reality of that place get away from me?*

With that thought, I looked up and saw another person with me in the tunnel. It was the child in the stained robe with the black hair. It twitched, slowly moving towards me in the distance. It danced on the border of my peripheral vision. Its skin was pale, and its hair ran like black vines down to its atrophied legs. The child's legs looked to be shaking under the weight of its emaciated frame. Its gown was just as tattered and filthy as the last time I encountered it. I was terrified, but I forced myself to face it. *It was only a child.*

As I turned to look at it straight on, it disappeared before my eyes. I paused.

That child had invaded my nightmares for years. I dreamt constantly about the terror I felt that night in the tunnel when it had approached me. I often awoke covered in sweat; I'm sure I had even wet the bed a time or two. But, each morning, I pushed it out of my thoughts and moved on with my day. *How was I able to ignore it?* I blinked, I think. The child was standing directly in front of me. The glint of light in its eye conveyed a familiar hatred that caused my chest to lock up and cut short my breath.

I tried so hard, for so long, to burn its image out of my memory with anything I could get my hands on. But there was no forgetting that night – not really. I had only locked it away in my subconscious for a while. The child was patient, just like *The Showers*. It waited in the back of my mind for my inevitable return.

I felt its breath against my face. It smelled like death. Long, stringy hair covered my eyes. I saw only the deep yellow of its eye. I shut my eyes tight and quickly opened them once again. I saw nothing.

There was no light down there, and my phone was gone. I couldn't have seen the child. It couldn't have been there. There was only darkness. My heart rate slowed once again. *It was only in my head.*

I felt around desperately for a wall. My hand brushed against cold sheet metal. It was brittle and rusted, but it was something solid – something tangible and real. I tried my best to work through my breathing exercises. I did everything I could to ground myself – tether myself to reality. I felt like I was slipping away.

My mind began aimlessly wandering down an existentially terrifying train of thought. I considered the idea that *The Showers* may not have existed before me. *Had I called it into existence? Was Mr. Mays just a kook who had inadvertently put me on a path toward manifesting that place? Was it a prison that I had constructed for myself – a tomb I was always meant to die in?*

My grip slipped from the wall. I stood in the darkness, swaying – swimming in it. I was overcome with a strange sense of relief. It felt like a blanket had wrapped itself around me. I felt warm. The hair on the back of my neck stood up.

All of my lies, half-truths, and made-up details about *The Showers* faded. I didn't need to hide from reality any longer. I was back in the place that had shattered the grasp that I thought I held on how the world worked, but it felt *good*. I laughed; I couldn't help myself. I'm sure it sounded like I was losing it. The situation seemed hilarious to me.

After graduating from college and visiting *The Showers* for the first time, I spent several years sleeping on couches and subletting rooms when I could find them. In that entire time, I never once saw an ounce of comfort. I never felt at ease. I was always restless, itching to be *somewhere else*. But I had no idea where that was. Somehow, I found a sense of familiarity in a hole in the ground in Nebraska – it felt like comfort enough.

That comfort came with a sense of freedom. I didn't have to lie to anyone, least of all to myself, or put on a mask for anyone. I felt like I didn't have to hold on so tightly anymore.

The Showers had become a part of me. As much distance as I had put between the two of us and as much as I had tried to push them away – to burn them out of my memory with force – they stuck with me. It felt like a homecoming. I could lose myself in peace there. I breathed normally for the first time in an eternity and let myself fall back into the warmth of the darkness.

My head caught the edge of a piece of sheet metal, tearing a hole in my scalp as I awkwardly smacked against the wall behind me. I was back in my body and quickly tried to reel my thoughts back in. I couldn't grasp what had just happened to me.

It was like the void called out for me to fill it, and my mind attempted to do just that. But, it let *everything* fly forth at once. There was too much space to fill. I spread so quickly across that empty mental plane that I came dangerously close to getting lost.

I was shaking uncontrollably. I tried my best to feel around me for something solid. There were bits of sheet metal, old wooden columns holding up the tunnel, and dirt. The goddamn ground was enough for me to keep myself present, in the moment, and out of wherever my head had just taken me. I made a promise to myself that I would go to get back on medication if I made it out of there. I had never felt so close to falling over the edge of sanity.

I began to move forward once again, making sure to keep a tight hold on something at all times. My hands were numb, but knowing that the walls were there – that the space around me was finite – was vital. The tunnels were physical; they were in the realm of the known. Anything outside of that was where the real horror waited.

A flash of bright red appeared in my peripheral vision. *How could I have forgotten that?* I turned to face the red door. It wouldn't have looked out of place on a model home in white suburbia, yet here it was – out of its element, just like me. Its floral pattern was as intricate as it had been years before. A skull-like face in the wood stared back at me with eyes like black pits. I breathed deeply and kept my hand on the wall. I knew I was imagining the door, but that didn't make it less real in the moment. Rationality didn't make it instantly disappear.

I felt a warm liquid run down the back of my head. It was blood from where the sheet metal had sliced open my scalp. I reached my hand back and ran my fingers along the wound, wincing from the pain. I pulled my hand away instinctively.

"Fuck!" I cried. I looked up, and the door was gone. I shut my eyes tightly once more. I needed to make sure it was in my head. I told myself over and over that when the brain is deprived of sight or sound, it will hallucinate to fill the gaps. *I was just under a lot of stress. None of it was real. I was in a hole in the ground in the middle of Nebraska, and I wasn't going to lose myself there.*

My eyes snapped open, and I saw only darkness. I breathed a sigh of relief.

As momentarily motivated as I might have been, the cold was getting to me. I tucked my hands under my arms and leaned against the wall. The blood on the back of my head had begun to freeze. My hair crackled as I leaned my head against the wall. I slowly began to slide down to the ground. *I just need to rest a minute.*

My eyelids gently lowered. It felt nice to rest.

After several seconds, I heard a faint voice in my ears. I wasn't quite sure if I had drifted off to sleep or if I was hallucinating again. It was Mr. Mays' voice. But, it wasn't comforting. It was not the joyful and calming voice he used in his classroom, but the dejected and drunken one from the last time I had seen him at the bar – the night I learned the truth about *The Showers*.

"That's a bad place, Jack," I heard him say. The liquor clung to his breath so heavily that night. I could almost smell it down in those tunnels like he was sitting in front of me once again. "Cops… drunk… *taken by wildlife.*" He slurred his words.

"Why would you want to go there?" I perked up. Mr. Mays had never asked me that question.

"It's a scary story. It's what *I do*," I responded out loud. I sat there in uncomfortable silence, unsure whether or not I should expect a response.

"It was *my* story, Jack – my own story," spoke Mr. Mays from within my head. "It was my goddamn *tragedy*, Jack. You wanted to see it for yourself? You wanted to have a cool story to impress your friends, right? Did you *really* want to live it?" I wasn't sure how to respond or if I even should. "Or did you just want to put yourself in the center of it?" he asked. "Always had to be at the story's center, didn't you? Well, here you are now, Jackie – *dead center.* How does it feel?"

"You're wrong!" I screamed. I slammed my fist into the wall next to me. There was a muffled *crack* as the brittle metal siding fractured. I had shaved the skin off of my knuckles. I felt the momentary warmth of blood running down my fingers.

The Showers taunted me, and I yelled out in anger. I needed a drink so badly I could taste it. But, through the blood and the cold, I couldn't get my hand into my jacket to grab my flask. I got so much blood on the zipper from simply trying to grip it that it froze up. I probably wouldn't have been able to open the flask anyway, so I gave up.

My memories – or some corrupted version of my memories – filled the seemingly endless darkness around me, and the only thing that I wanted at that moment was for them to quiet down so I could hear myself think. I pushed back against the wall and up to my feet. I took one step forward and hit my shoulder on a wooden beam which sent me right back onto my ass. I slumped down on my side in defeat. That was what it wanted, that place, even though it couldn't *want.*

"I did this to myself," I thought, unsure if I was speaking out loud. "I wrote this ending for myself when I went chasing *The Showers* for my own gain and posted about it on the internet. I built this extension of myself – this monster." My head rested on the dirt. "Now it's consuming me, slowly – digesting me."

The Showers was just a hole in the ground in motherfucking Nebraska that I used to dump my fears into. I made them into what they had become. I had let them grow into my personal hell.

"I let this happen," I said. "I did this to myself."

The room began to quiet. I felt the space shrinking around me.

"Fucking hell on Earth, if you ask me," a voice rang in my ears. It was Mr. Mays again, but it wasn't taunting me. It was something he had actually told me about Broken Bow way back when. I could never say that the guy didn't warn me.

When I heard that quote in those tunnels—head on the dirt in a slowly freezing pool of my own blood—I became acutely aware of the hint of sadness and fear in Mr. Mays' voice that I had never noticed before.

I let my eyes close again, not that it mattered much in the dark. I walked myself slowly through the truth I had likely always known but never addressed.

Mr. Mays was just a tired old man. He had a traumatic experience in his younger years, and he lost a friend. The situation was as simple as that. Maybe the cops found his friend's body, and maybe they didn't; the details didn't really matter. His friend was dead, and Mr. Mays didn't have the tools to cope with that kind of trauma. He drank himself to death to shrink his agony down to a manageable size. It just needed to be small enough to hide away and check on during *really* rough nights every now and then. Maybe he succeeded for a little while. But that trauma was still a silent driving force behind every last action that he took. It didn't even matter whether or not he was conscious of that fact. He woke up with it every single morning. He dragged it through each and every day. Then, he drank until he forgot about it for a few precious hours. But it would always be there when he woke up the following day, ready to go another round. Over time, that weight warped him. It turned his core black and tainted every aspect of his life in some way.

One day, he was gone. The only legacy he left behind was a scary story about the poison that slowly killed him.

I heard a creaking sound above me and felt a drop of cold liquid hit my shoulder and splash lightly on my face. Another voice quickly stole my attention.

"J-Jack," the voice stuttered, cutting through the silence. My heartbeat raced. My brain was still reeling from everything I had encountered since entering the tunnel, so it took me a second to process who was speaking.

"It was Karen," I thought to myself. "Karen is a person. Karen is my girlfriend. Karen went into the tunnel. I went after Karen. We are both in the tunnel now. Karen just spoke."

"Karen," I said out loud, carefully pushing myself off the ground. "Follow my voice. Come closer to me. Come ov–"

"You were talking to yourself," she interrupted. Her voice was soft, and she sounded scared. "You were talking to yourself like you do in your sleep." I ignored her comment.

"Just come to me, please," I said.

"This place...I should have believed you," Karen whimpered. "What the hell is down here, Jack?"

"I don't know," I told her.

"Bullshit," she said. "You *do* know, so just tell me! Stop fucking lying!" I could hear her begin to cry. "I'm scared, Jack."

"I'm so sorry, Karen," I said, struggling. "I can't explain this. Please just come over here." She didn't respond. I sighed and opened my mouth wide to crack my jaw. Each *pop* rippled through my skull. There was a dull shot of pain in my temples, but it felt like relief. I had nothing to lose anymore; I had to be honest with Karen about *The Showers*. All it took was for us to get stuck in a sub-ground waking nightmare for me to get to that point.

"I don't know what this place is or what it did to me," I said, trying to find the right words. "But, I wasn't the same after I came here. It fucked me up. *I'm* fucked up. I don't know why, and I don't know how to fix it. But I never wanted you to go through what I did. I was afraid. Look at this place," I gestured all around me; neither of us saw it.

"I could have helped you," she said quietly. Her use of the past tense stung. I heard her either move towards me or rest against the nearest wall.

"How?" I asked. Silence filled the space between us for a few drawn-out seconds.

"We could have shared it." I could hear the tears in her voice. "We could have shared the weight, Jack." I was almost speechless.

"Well," I said, "we're sharing it now."

The walls groaned around us. The noise moved quickly around the room, settling right above me. I looked up and into the dark.

"What's that?" Karen said. "It sounds like–"

Ice-cold water rained onto me from above, instantly soaking me from head to toe.

I gasped hard, taking in a deep breath and some of the liquid along with it while my every muscle tensed up from the shock and the cold. The taste of rust filled my mouth. Before I could think about it for too long, my body acted without me—coughing and sputtering to rid my lungs of the tainted water. I fell back to my knees.

Despite the complete lack of light, I knew exactly what hung a couple of feet above my head. I wanted nothing more than to be out of that place, but I didn't move from underneath the showerhead. I looked up and let the freezing rain pour directly onto my face; I let it swallow me.

Another deep rumble emanated from within the walls around me, and Karen screamed. Water splashed onto the ground from my left, right, in front of me, and then behind. Still, I sat there while my hands pruned and my arms lost feeling. I felt my breath turn to ice as it left my lungs. Despite the extremity of the situation, I felt a warm calmness from within. I slowly spread my arms out at my sides. If ice water was all that *The Showers* held for me, I thought I might be okay.

The showerheads rained down around me, and there was a symphony of crystal clear noise from the creaking pipes to the dull splatter of each droplet of liquid as it hit the ground. Every sound was clear and full. The noise almost illuminated the room. I took it all in; I accepted it. If *The Showers* wanted me, I was ready to go. I had made a pilgrimage to the place that birthed the subhuman thing I had become over the previous several years, and I was prepared to give up. If it wanted me back, I wasn't going to fight.

I could hear Karen scream my name from only feet away, but she was drowned out by the noise. Most of my body was numb, yet I still felt a stinging under my skin with every last drop of water.

A sense of instability—vertigo-like—began to overtake me. I opened my eyes, and, to my surprise, they were filled with bright light.

I was back in Mr. Mays' classroom. It looked the same as it had so many years ago, complete with Halloween decorations and drawn shades. I stood at the front of the class, looking down over the thirty teenage faces that stared back at me. The faces were blurred as if out of focus. It was my classroom; those were my students.

"How did you get out of the tunnel?" a distorted voice asked from the crowd.

"I…I don't know," I responded.

I blinked, and my environment changed. I was in the dimly lit tunnels. I was helping carry my friend Steve, who first ventured to this place with me years ago, away from the approaching darkness behind us. He was bleeding from a head wound. The event seemed *wrong*.

"This isn't how it happened," I cried between breaths. "This isn't *my* story." I passed an open red door on my right. My faceless students sat in the classroom beyond the doorway. I jumped past the threshold, pulling Steve with me.

I landed on a bed in a dark room. I sat up immediately. Sweat soaked my sheets, and tears soaked my face. I sank my face into my hands, and I shook my head. I knew that what I was seeing couldn't be real. I thought I might have slipped beyond; I thought I was dead and that what I was seeing was what I would spend eternity reliving. I would spend my time in purgatory, trapped within *The Showers*.

I pulled my hands away from my face and found myself at a bar. Next to me sat Mr. Mays. He was smiling.

"One more for the road, please," he said to the bartender. "One for Jackie here, too."

Within seconds, we each had a triple shot of some kind of brown liquor sitting before us. I looked up at Mr. Mays. I went to speak, but my voice froze in my throat. I wanted to say something, but a cloud of visible breath was all that came out of my mouth. Mr. Mays downed his drink in a single gulp and looked at me.

"You need to get out of there, Jack," he said. "So how are you gonna do it?" I gave him a desperate, unsure look. "There's no sense in us both going down because of this fucking place." Mr. Mays placed a reassuring hand on my shoulder. "So, go on. Tell me how the hell you're planning on escaping." He looked into my eyes and grabbed my drink. I tried to speak once more, but my chest locked up. I reached towards him. My hand dripped with water. My fingers had turned purple.

"Ah, playing it close to the chest," he said. "I get it. I get it." He winked at me and threw the shot back. "Just make it a good story, eh?" He nodded and grinned. "Cheers to you, Jack."

The bar went dark.

A dull, wet *thump* rang out a few feet to my left, snapping me back to my body. Karen had fallen and screamed my name, which rang out loudly above the noise of the water.

"Jack, what's going on!?" she screamed as I heard her body drag across the muddy floor away from me.

I could hardly feel my frozen extremities, so I threw myself on the ground in the direction of her voice and began to crawl forward as fast as I could. I wasn't going to let that place have her; I wasn't going to let it have me. We were going to get out of the darkness.

I reached my arm out as far as I could towards Karen's screams despite being unable to feel much of it. My arm fell across her shoulder in a rare stroke of good fortune. She immediately grabbed me. I closed my hand around part of her denim jacket as tightly as I could. I pulled her close and wrapped my legs around her. She wrapped her arms around me and buried her head in my chest. Her screams were only slightly muffled. I let her have that moment of release. I didn't know what else to do. I held her tightly and looked out into the darkness surrounding us. I don't know exactly what I was looking for.

Her screams turned to quiet sobs as the water pressure from the showerheads audibly died down, eventually stopping. We lay there together in the freezing mud for a few minutes. Eventually, Karen's sobs quieted.

"W-we need t-t-to stand up, okay?" I stuttered, frozen. I loosened the vice grip I had on her and stumbled to my feet. I didn't let myself lose contact with her for a moment. She rose to meet me. We stayed as close together as possible. I had no idea where we were in relation to anything else in the tunnels. "We got-ta f-f-find a wall." We locked arms and moved to my right.

After ten long and careful steps, I hit a wall. I couldn't tell if it was covered in ice or if I was just so numb that I couldn't feel the coarse cement. Karen kept her head against my shoulder. I started to feel emotional—angry that she had forced me to come back to this place. The anger turned quickly to sadness when I realized that she was going to have to carry the weight of that place with her for the rest of her life. I felt guilty for letting it happen. I muttered to myself under my breath. I knew I could have stopped the trip if I had tried harder; I could have stopped mentioning *The Showers* long before it reached that point. But I didn't. The whole situation was my fault.

The pipes groaned inside the wall next to us. With each subsequent sound, I felt my stomach clench in preparation for another blast of ice water. I didn't think I could stand anymore at that point. I figured that I would be lucky to make it out of that place with only light frostbite. In contrast with the numbness throughout my body, my jaw throbbed in pain. I couldn't unclench my teeth; they felt like they would break apart like crushed ice. I wanted to give up right there. I was so tired and so afraid. I wasn't the kind of person who would save his girlfriend and come out of those tunnels a changed man. I didn't even think we were going to get out at all. But I pushed on for Karen.

I was lost in thought, putting most of my weight against the wall as I slid along it. I was bracing for sharp corners when my shoulder found an abrupt, empty space. I caught one hand on the corner of the wall as I fell, but that did very little when my feet gave way in the mud beneath me. I fell face down into the wet slop. My free hand landed under my hip. It let out a *crack* and a *pop*. I screamed into the mud. Karen screamed back. I rolled over and brought my hand carefully up to my face. The angles of my fingers seemed utterly wrong when I rubbed them against my cheek. They were undoubtedly broken.

After a time, we became too exhausted and out of breath to continue screaming. I focused on my breathing and tried to ignore my mangled hand. I sat up, pushing my good hand through the icy mud, and eased myself onto my feet. Something grazed my fingers while it was planted in the mud. It was smooth, but not like cement—like metal. It was small. I gripped it as best I could as I stood up. My legs wobbled. I was getting the spins but couldn't tell if it was from the booze, the concussion, or the disorienting darkness. Karen got to my side quick enough and stabilized me. She pulled herself close.

"I'm sorry. We shouldn't have come here. I didn't believe you," she cried in between quick breaths.

I didn't want an apology. I wanted to scream at her and take her straight to bed at the same time. I wanted to be anywhere else, fighting with her about something stupid and irrelevant. The space around us filled with a mess of conflicting emotions amidst my silence. Karen eventually broke the tension.

"What d-do you have in your hand?" she asked.

I managed to keep hold of the object I had discovered in the mud. We both felt around it, desperately trying to get a sense of what it was. It could have just been a piece of one of the showerheads for all we knew, but for a second, there was hope that it was a solution. It was sort of cylindrical. It was mostly metal. It had a little clip on it. I rolled it around in my hand, careful not to drop it. It had a button. I recognized it before I could turn it on. It was a small flashlight – the kind hikers fastened to their backpacks.

"F-f-flashlight," I stuttered. My fingertips could feel the button but couldn't quite press it hard enough. "Help m-me push the s-switch." Karen traced along my fingers with her own and found it. She pressed it in.

The light was hardly blinding. We were prepared to shield our eyes but were surprised by its weakness. It did little to help our situation, but it did something. Once our eyes had adjusted, we could see the showerheads in our immediate area. The whole enclosure looked and smelled like a pigsty, and we couldn't see an exit.

The loud wailing of a dying animal came from nowhere and quickly enveloped us. It felt like we had accidentally stood in front of a mass of speakers at a concert. My head pulsated, and I felt my ribs vibrate. Karen covered her ears with her frozen hands. The tips of her fingers were bright red, maybe even purple. It was hard to tell from the weak light of the flashlight.

The noise itself rang out without letting up. It started as a high-pitched, organic whine but, over the course of thirty seconds, distorted into something that better resembled a foghorn.

Karen wrapped her arms around me. I held her head against my chest.

"Close your eyes. Just keep them closed," I told Karen.

I kept the beam centered on us as much as I could. It didn't bother me that whatever was out there could see us. The light provided some sort of warmth or, at the very least, a sense of solidity. The noise slowly died down until we were left once again in silence.

"W-we have to move back to the tunnel. You h-h-have to help me find it," I said, trying to get us back on track.

Karen nodded, tearing her face away from my chest. Her tears had frozen her cheek to my sweater. I could see a rim of ice around the red mark on her cheek.

"Back that way, I think," she said, pointing to a wall on our left. I couldn't tell where exactly we had come from. The light didn't do much to penetrate the darkness, and even then, we were moving in the dark, so we had no visual markers to go by. But I trusted her. We began to shuffle through the mud, which was now a slushy consistency. It seeped into my boots. Every inch of my body was covered in water and frost; a little more cold couldn't hurt.

Every few steps, the flashlight would dim or flicker. I could feel Karen tense up every time I gave it a shake. I was rolling the dice on how long it would continue to help us, but I did my best to keep calm and on track.

Inevitably, it went out completely. Karen dug her fingers into my side. I shook the light; the battery inside rattled around. Nothing happened. I hit against the palm of my injured hand several times. Nothing happened.

"Please work. Please," I muttered to myself as I hit the switch off and on several times in rapid succession. I couldn't let it go; it was all we had down in those tunnels, the only thing keeping us from the all-consuming darkness. I didn't want to go back to that. After a few more attempts, there was light. However, it was coming from all the way across the room.

An exposed bulb, maybe forty feet across the room from us, came to life. It was dim but enough to light up a significant portion of the space in front of it.

About ten feet in front of the bulb and thirty feet from us stood the silhouette of a massive buck. Its head bent down towards the ground. It had a large set of antlers - twelve points, if I had to guess. Karen's breathing quickened, and I felt her hot breath against my neck. I struggled to grasp what I saw and let the dead flashlight fall from my hands to the ground. We both jumped slightly as it hit the ground with one last flash of the bulb. The metal slapped against the cement, and the tiny bit of glass cracked like a stick snapping under a foot in the woods.

The buck tensed up and rose to attention. Its antlers scraped hard against the low ceiling. Some of the points were only grinding against it, while others cracked and broke off entirely. By all accounts, the animal should have been in immense pain, but it didn't even seem to notice—at the very least, it didn't seem to care. As it turned its attention towards us, Karen tugged hard on my sweater.

"We h-ha-have to get out. K-k-keep moving," Karen cried quietly. We continued down the path before us while the buck let out a cry like the noise we had heard before. A jolt of pain shot through my temples. The noise went on continuously – one long whine that should have been interrupted by a breath at some point but just kept going. By the end, it had become something more reminiscent of a foghorn. I looked behind us as we shuffled through the dark. A hint of yellow light reflected off the eye of the beast. It was looking directly at me; it was tracking me. I turned my head and heard several other bulbs click and come to life on the far side of the room. I didn't look back.

A door came into view in front of us. The paint was stripped. The wood was aged and cracked from years of weathering. Even still, I was able to get a sense of the brilliant shade of red that used to cover it. The floral pattern had withered away, leaving only the deeply etched tree and the outline of a skeletal face at its base. The dark pits still looked like eyes to me. Crudely carved into its forehead was a single word: *Twigs*. I didn't take any time to think about what it meant. The door's knocker was missing a screw, and it hung limply off-center. The knob still had some shine to it—I could see the reflection of the lights behind us in it as we moved closer. I went to reach my hand out to grasp the knob, but Karen had already beaten me to it. She grabbed it and twisted. The internal metal mechanisms shifted loudly, quieting the bleating of the buck in the distance. Even after Karen peeled her hand from the frozen metal, the door cracked and creaked.

The wood started to split. Deep cracks spread rapidly outwards from the knob, crawling across the wood until they reached the hinges. The door shifted and began to tip downward. I didn't think I had the strength to stop it. It started to tilt. I raised my arm to shield Karen's head while trying to pull us out of the way. It caught abruptly on the old screws in its middle and lower hinges and swung to the left – right in front of us. I felt the rush of cold air as it brushed within an inch of my face and slammed into the wall. It fell to the ground and sunk into the mud.

Through the open doorway, I could make out the beginning of a familiar tunnel. The ceiling rose and sank abruptly like the hills of a roller coaster. Some spots had no more than three feet of clearance from top to bottom when I had been there last. But, at that moment, when we needed the tunnel the most, there was no clearance at all. The metal sheets that held the earth at bay had given way. The tunnel had collapsed. I realized then that the property could have tens of tunnels all around it for all I knew; the place could have been a maze. We didn't need a maze or the hope of another exit. We were at our wit's end and needed that tunnel to be our exit. Hope drained from my body.

"Fuck!" I screamed, exhausted. My lungs burned. My mind was on fire. Every motion I made was out of instinct. I couldn't properly process what was happening around me.

Neither of us turned around. We stood before the doorway and stared at the caved-in tunnel that had sealed our fate. I grabbed Karen's hand and held onto it tightly as more lights flickered to life behind us. I'm sure there were other exits in that room, but the uncertainty of what we might see stopped us from moving. We just looked forward and stayed frozen in place.

I heard the hard clapping of a set of hooves against the ground somewhere in the room – then another. I saw shadows of what were unmistakably humans shrinking as they moved towards us. It was the children; I was sure of it. Even amidst the overwhelming stench, I could smell them—pennies and vinegar. Their robes dragged across the mud and their hair covered their bodies, skewing the proportions in their shadows. Karen gripped my hand tighter. Two shadows moved along the walls, then five, ten, and I lost count.

The bulbs near us came to life and caused the frost that had built up on the cement walls to melt. Each new light source caused the shadows to fade further; each new light left us increasingly unsure of what exactly approached us. A few of the children appeared to have antlers mounted atop their heads.

A bulb mounted only a couple of feet to my right flickered on.

On my left, Karen's head turned upward. There, protruding several feet from the wall, was a showerhead. It looked fragile and old, rusty, and caked with glistening frost. With her free hand, she reached up, grabbed hold of the pipe, and pulled down, squeezing my hand as if she were using me for leverage. It broke off with surprising ease. Karen pulled back as water sprayed into the room behind us from the broken pipe. I could hear feet skitter through the mud and away from the torrent of ice. Karen turned towards me – eyes closed – and buried her face in my arm. She presented the showerhead to me like a weapon.

I carefully took the rusted metal in my injured hand. It had a surprising weight to it. I gripped as tightly as I could despite the pain from my fingers. For the first time in those tunnels, I felt like I had *some* control. The footsteps around us grew closer, picking up speed. I looked toward the bulb on my right.

"Fuck this place," I said as I swung the pipe through the air. It smashed through the bulb with ease. The pain in my hand caused me to loosen my grip, and the pipe flew through the air just along the wall, breaking two more bulbs as it went. Shattered glass rained onto the mud as, to my surprise, the other lights in the room began to extinguish. One by one, the room fell back into darkness.

I heard the animalistic scream – the foghorn – once more. The footsteps behind us had grown very close. They couldn't have been more than a few feet from us. I hugged Karen as tightly as possible as the last bulb went out. There we stood in the darkness again, surrounded by the unknown. I hadn't considered until then whether it would be better to die in the dark or the light.

I kissed Karen on the head, keeping a tight hold on her as I turned to face the room.

The bulbs had died, but the filaments still had a slight glow – like the aftermath of a camera flash. As my eyes adjusted, I could make out silhouettes of the children. Some were no more than an arm's length away. There were tiny dots of light in their eyes, and they all pointed directly at me. The air was filled with a familiar, tangible anger; I could feel their hatred. They seemed to hate me as much as I feared them. I couldn't even guess what would happen once they got a hold of us. I just prayed that it would be over quickly and that the fear would cease at the very least. The filaments in the bulbs dimmed and died. The darkness settled. I closed my eyes.

"I'm sorry," I spoke into the top of Karen's head. The children were right on us. I felt a cold breath on the back of my neck. I gripped Karen tighter. Fingernails lightly grazed my cheeks. I could feel my hands grasping at my clothes. I clenched up in anticipation. The thought of jumping from a bridge came to mind. It sounded peaceful compared to the end I was facing.

I let out one last breath as I felt the hands tighten their grip around my wrists and ankles.

Without warning, it stopped. The hands loosened their grip and pulled away. The breathing on the back of my neck ceased. Feet flew through the mud, away from us. The children were fleeing. The foghorn noise stopped abruptly. In seconds, the room had settled into a peaceful silence.

It felt like a trick.

After the goosebumps on my neck faded, I gathered the courage to open one eye. I looked upward. About ten feet in front of us was a ray of bright light. It was powerful, cutting through the dark like a beacon. Even at a distance, the frost on Karen's bright red hair sparkled. I had no idea where the light was coming from. Briefly, I considered that I was entirely wrong about religion and that it was some sort of divine intervention. Then, I heard the familiar growl of a car engine. My eyes adjusted, and I could see the light coming from a hole in the ceiling where wooden boards had collapsed long ago.

I couldn't fucking believe it.

I didn't say a word as the car door slammed, and Brian stepped towards the hole.

"Hello down there!" his voice rang out like music to my ears. Karen looked up and immediately broke away from me. There was a sense of relief in her eyes, but her face was frozen in shock. She moved quickly.

"Brian," her voice croaked. "Brian, you get us out of this fucking hole right now, and I will buy you your own grow house."

"I am gonna hold you to that, Kare-bear." He laughed.

I assumed they could see each other at that point. Karen glared towards the hole. She was bathed in light. I slowly began to move towards her. My knee popped, and my joints ached. I was dizzy and confused but pretty confident that I wasn't hallucinating. It felt unlikely, but it felt real.

"Okay, but it's not gonna be easy," said Brian. "I found a rope. It's kind of icy, but I don't have another option, and I'm still a little high, so it will have to work. How the hell did you guys get down there?" Karen didn't answer as Brian dropped an old purple climber's rope. She grabbed it and began to ascend like her life depended on it. Brian was grunting from above and jokingly commenting on how she had gained weight. She was out of the hole within seconds, and I was left alone.

I looked around me. The space was smaller than it had seemed just minutes ago. The walls were cracked. The mud was turning back to solid ice. There wasn't a single sign of life. *The Showers* were still and empty.

"You coming, Jack?" asked Brian as I finally made it under the hole. I grabbed the rope tightly and looked behind me towards the decrepit red door that barely stuck out of the mud. In the tunnel behind it, I could make out the dark silhouette of someone standing just beyond the reach of the light. A quick jolt of fear shot through me. But after staring directly at the figure for several seconds, the fear subsided. I turned away from it and didn't look back.

With some help from Brian, I pulled myself out of the hole and onto the frozen ground outside. It had started to snow. I took deep breaths of fresh air, like water in the desert; it had never felt so refreshing. I was free of the stench of that place, but my stomach was still in knots.

The moon reflected off the snow and ice, lighting up the clearing around us. I could see Karen pacing behind the car. She was staying close to the tail lights. She stopped suddenly and fixed her vision on the edge of the trees with a terrified look on her face. Reality began to sink in. Karen would have to live with that experience for the rest of her life, and that would always be my fault.

I was on the verge of tears when Brian helped me to my feet. I still hadn't entirely decompressed. My jaw still clenched tightly shut. I could feel the remnants of one of my chipped front teeth embedded in my gum. I didn't remember breaking it. Every part of my body felt numb. My clothes were frozen to my skin. But, I couldn't rest until we had gotten out of there – all the way out.

Karen began to scream.

"It's right there! It's right there!" she yelled. As she screamed, she pointed towards the trees. Brian dropped everything and ran towards her. I slumped down and stared at the ground. I felt that there was nothing that I could do for Karen. I was as much of a mess as she was.

Her cries blended into the background as my mind returned to Mr. Mays. I wondered what he would have done in that situation. But he *had* been there; I knew exactly what his solution was, and it didn't seem like a bad idea for now. I reached into my jacket pocket, pulled out the flask, opened it, and sniffed. To my surprise, it burned my nostrils like gasoline. It made me nauseous. I looked down at the flask. Karen had it engraved for me on Valentine's Day the year before. The engraving read: *May love and liquor light your life. Always yours, Karen.*

I closed it and looked behind me at the hole in the ground.

I tossed the flask down into the dark. I didn't hear it hit the bottom.

"Cheers," I said under my breath.

I stood up and walked towards Karen, whose cries were becoming increasingly sporadic. She jumped at her shadow as a confused and stoned Brian tried to help her.

"Man, what the hell is going on with her?!" he asked.

"Make sure the car is ready to go," I told him. I passed him by without making eye contact. Karen saw me coming and froze. I took her hands and held them in my own.

"Jack, *how* was it like that?! How were *they* like that? *Why* was *any* of that–" she rambled, unsure of what she had seen and what she wanted to ask. Eventually, she broke down completely. "It doesn't make *any fucking sense*! I didn't *know*. I *didn't know*. I didn't *know*." She bawled, and I held her there. It was all that I could do at the time. She slammed her fists against my chest out of frustration a few times. I let her get it out. I didn't know how to help her. But I could be a punching bag; I could take it.

After she had calmed down, I eased her over to the car and sat her in the back seat. I wrapped her in as many blankets as possible and buckled her in. As I walked around to the other side of the car, I looked back at the hole in the ground one last time. Snow had already started covering the tracks we had made while climbing out. I turned away and got into the car.

Brian drove through the trees as quickly as he could. He had managed to get the car around the massive, dead tree to get to us—no doubt tearing up my paint job in the process. But I was thankful. We retraced his path to get out of there.

A few times, Brian seemed to begin a question but stopped himself. He told us how he had been in the car when he saw a light coming from the ground and what he thought was one of us waving him over. Neither Karen nor I reacted to his story. A weight hung over the two of us. Brian quickly picked up on that fact and stayed quiet. Questions could wait. I'm not sure if he ever actually got around to them.

Karen wasn't asleep in the backseat, but her eyes were closed tightly.

I was buzzing as we drove away. It wasn't until we crossed the threshold of the tree line and found ourselves back on a real rural road that I could loosen the vice grip I had held on the door handle. The electricity shooting through my nerves faded as the stars overtook the tops of the trees surrounding *The Showers*. Only then did my insides begin to relax. The dam holding my emotions during the trip finally began to burst. I asked Brian to pull over. He obliged almost immediately and without a word.

I stumbled out of the car and began throwing up on the side of the road. Thick, yellowish bile hung in the back of my throat before slowly dripping down and out of my body. It felt like what I deserved. I gagged and felt my eyes bulge as I purged. I clawed at my stomach, sore from the continuous heaving over the previous day or more. I clenched my fist and hit the ground, causing the wounds on my knuckles to open. Only then did I take a look at my injured hand. My middle and ring fingers were broken; it looked like someone had taken a bottle opener to my nail and first knuckle. I shouldn't have just left them that way, but I didn't get much reprieve before I had to bow and purge again.

It was the tail end of an exorcism. What felt like years' worth of stress, lies, and fear violently erupted from within me until my lips numbed, my stomach slowly relaxed, and my ears loudly popped. The *pop* instantly relieved most of the pressure on the inside of my skull. I felt like I was floating. I was crying, and I knew why, but I couldn't quite isolate my individual thoughts. It all became a messy cloud of *feelings.* The world around me felt foreign. Everything in my brain was misfiring; it was rebooting.

My only coherent thought was, "I made it out."

I sat in the dirt long enough that my vomit turned to slush on the ground in front of me. Brian stayed in the car and looked in the other direction. I think I felt Karen's hand on my back at one point. But when I had finished, she was in the car staring anywhere else but at me.

I collapsed into the vehicle, shaking and soaking wet. Brian started to drive off before I had even shut the door. I saw Karen's lip tremble several times, but she said nothing. I don't know how she managed that. It felt like we *needed* to talk about what had happened. But communication was never our strong suit. I caught her looking at me only once on the drive back as we passed by the exit for Broken Bow.

We forgave each other for the things that happened that night, though neither of us ever said it out loud. We didn't talk about *The Showers* much at all. We filled that place with exactly what we brought there – pain and truths about ourselves that we were using each other to hide from. The horror we experienced was a dose of – as Karen put it so many times before – *perspective.* It woke us up from the fever dream that our lives had become.

I think we both realized – painfully sobering up over the six-hour car ride back home and staring straight out of the windshield without actually seeing – that we were better off apart.

Similar to how she had moved into my apartment, we never *really* discussed her moving out; her things just started disappearing over the following two weeks. We repeated the old mantra about "staying friends" for another week or so, but you could practically hear it echo every time one of us said it. We knew that we were just parroting an empty sentiment at each other. With a soft kiss on my cheek on a Thursday afternoon, she was out of my life.

Karen and I couldn't work because we fit too well together. We were two uniquely fucked up individuals with a penchant for flipping on a dime and a need for a partner to share in our mutual misery. It's easy to look back and long for those nights cuddling and watching movies together on the couch. It's a lot harder to remember reality. There were nights spent cuddling on the couch and going out with friends that I occasionally miss. But, with a little effort, I can now push through that façade and remember how many of those nights ended in shouting matches, broken dishes, and tears. That was almost every night for us: a perfect couple and a perpetual potential domestic dispute rolled into one. Our solution was to rinse the bad parts down and repeat. We were our own perfect enablers, and we were always heading towards the end that we got. Broken Bow did nothing but illuminate what was already in front of us: the reality of our codependence and the inevitability of our end.

I think I really did love her, for what that's worth. I genuinely hope she's doing better now.

As for me, I couldn't continue to live the way I was after Nebraska. I was completely covered in dirt and blood when we left *The Showers*. When we finally made it to a gas station, I looked at myself in the mirror and realized how far I had let myself spiral downward. I didn't drink or get high for kicks. I did both things because I was broken and needed something to fill the cracks. I realized that I couldn't use *The Showers* as an excuse forever; I couldn't keep lying to myself.

If that sounds like it came from the mouth of a therapist, it's because it did. I started going to therapy once every week, initially for the drinking but eventually for everything else. I'm not a religious convert or a friend of Bill, but I respect the journey and anyone willing to take it, no matter the method needed to make it through. I wish Mr. Mays had found a way to fight his demons before he left. I guess they're our demons, really. Hopefully, I can rid us of both of them.

I'm always going to carry *The Showers* with me. They are a part of who I am, but I don't have to let them kill me anymore.

The most important concept that I have learned in these therapy sessions is that you can't "get better" if you just keep covering up symptoms while ignoring the real source of your unhappiness. Blowing your brain out every night with substances just puts off the inevitable confrontation. You have to treat it like a wart; you have to cut all the way down to the root and tear it out to get rid of it; you have to get every last piece.

That is why I came back to this forum, this account, and this story. So many others out there listened to Mr. Mays' campfire story throughout the years and then moved on like ordinary people. I fixated, spread it, and put myself into the story because I couldn't resist. I did so without considering the potential fallout that comes with trying to emulate someone's trauma just for a fucking story. I was careless; I was stupid. After a lot of work, I have found a way to navigate this path I set myself on many years ago. I can now live on my own – separate from *The Showers*.

I can't un-write my original story; I can never put this genie back in the bottle. I can, however, try to control the narrative – or at least confuse it. I also understand that writing this seems to defeat the purpose of separating myself from that place. But this isn't what you might think it is. This is my last self-indulgent venture into the past, my farewell letter to Broken Bow, Nebraska, and whatever secrets *The Showers* might keep. There is a point to all of this.

The story is yours now; I don't *need* it anymore. Either *The Showers* die here with this post and eventually fade with time, or I let them go, and they survive on their own merits as an urban legend. Either way, they will do so without me.

So, take *The Showers* and mold them to your needs. Tell the story around a campfire and embellish whatever you'd like. Put yourself in the story, or a friend, or a friend of a friend, and then use it to get laid. Take your wildest theories about the place and create a story all your own. Make a movie or a book out of them. Turn them into a local urban legend in your own town. Be careful or be careless; it doesn't matter much to me. Just drown my story out with your own.

In fact, go there if you want. Go find *The Showers*. Ask every citizen in Broken Bow, Nebraska, about them until they run you out of town. Get lost on dirt roads a few miles east of the city until you stumble upon a place resembling the one I have described, and then tear it apart. Bring your friends and take pictures, explore the tunnels, light a bonfire, get drunk, throw a party, and then post about it on the internet. Cover the walls in graffiti and the floors with cigarette butts, broken bottles, and condom wrappers. Tell everyone you know about it. Flood the internet with so much speculation and rampant bullshit about that place that no one will ever point back to me as the source.

Drown me in the noise, or let me fade away in peace.

You can go there yourself and burn it all if you want. Just don't forget to tell everyone how you did it afterward.

Well, *shit*.

I let that go on for so long; that wasn't my intention. Old habits die hard. I've been pulling from a dusty flask of whiskey I found next to the laptop in the box; I guess it counts as "aged" now. I'm not really on any wagon, and after the years of bullshit I put my body through, I figure a few more nips aren't going to hurt a thing.

This is just one more for the road.

I didn't mean what I said.

If you go there, please be careful. Take a second and think about what you might be getting into. As a child, I found it exciting to insert myself into the scary stories I told the kids at school. It gave my stories an extra dose of reality, but was risky. If I didn't tell the *exact* same story every time, someone might call my bluff. I didn't realize at the time how dangerous it was to put myself into *someone else's* story – to attempt to live another person's trauma like I did with Mr. Mays. I didn't realize how easy it is to get caught up in these tales – to use them as a shield to hide from the horrors of your past.

When you put yourself into a story – whatever your reason for it – you bind yourself to it. It becomes a part of you. Truth and fiction blurs, ultimately becoming inconsequential. If you aren't paying close attention, it's easy to lose track of the narrative and – with that – lose track of yourself. The disconnect is the key; spin whatever narrative you want, but remember to keep your distance – keep grounded. Separating yourself from a story – if you're lucky enough to catch onto the damage before it consumes you – takes a heavy toll.

I didn't come out the same person I was before all of this. I sure as hell hurt some people I cared for by dragging them into my personal horror show. I'm sorry for whatever that's worth this late in the game.

I suppose that's enough of my rambling for one sitting.

I'm going to post this, log out of my account, tear up the sticky note I saved with my password written on it, shut down this laptop for what I hope to be the last time, and bury it back under all of the junk in my closet alongside this flask.

Tomorrow, I will go into my classroom at the community college, where I now teach a creative writing course. I will walk through those doors with a renewed sense of purpose and weight off of my shoulders. I will sit down and tell my students one of the many variations of *The Showers* I have told over the years. The version I tell those students won't be *my* story anymore. No, I'll tell them a version about my best friend's brother's ex-girlfriend and set it in some rural part of Pennsylvania a few years back. I'll make up new characters, places, and details as I see fit because I'm in control of the narrative now – not the other way around. It isn't Halloween yet, but maybe I'll dim the lights and burn a candle or two for atmosphere like Mr. Mays did for my class so many years ago.

I can't take back what I did when I posted this story years ago for the world to see. I'm not exactly sure that I would want to. So, instead, I'll take a page from my younger self and spread this like I'm playing a large-scale game of telephone – one that I intentionally wish to distort. Hell, it might even be fun.

I gave you a story on some dark night five years ago, and the only thing I am asking in return is for you to take it from me. Make it into something scarier or more violent, more cerebral or more personal; give it a twist ending. Make it *yours*.

My hope is that one day, someone will tell me their version of the story – with new faces, details, and scares – and that I won't recognize it until I hear the name that will forever haunt other's dreams instead of my own:

The Showers.